TWICE HEXED

Teas & Temptations Cozy Mysteries
Book Two

CINDY STARK

www.cindystark.com

Cover Design by Kelli Ann Morgan
Inspire Creative Services

License Notes

This ebook is licensed for your personal enjoyment only. This ebook may not be re-sold or given away to other people. If you would like to share this book with another person, please purchase an additional copy for each recipient. If you're reading this book and did not purchase it, or it was not purchased for your use only, then please purchase your own copy. The ebook contained herein constitutes a copyrighted work and may not be reproduced, transmitted, downloaded, or stored in or introduced into an information storage and retrieval system in any form or by any means, whether electronic or mechanical, now known or hereinafter invented, without the express written permission of the copyright owner, except in the case of brief quotation embodied in critical articles and reviews. Thank you for respecting the hard work of this author.

This ebook is a work of fiction. The names, characters, places, and incidents are products of the writer's imagination or have been used fictitiously and are not to be construed as real. Any resemblance to persons, living or dead, actual events, locales or organizations is entirely coincidental.

Welcome to Stonebridge, Massachusetts

Welcome to Stonebridge, a small town in Massachusetts where the label "witch" is just as dangerous now as it was in 1692. From a distance, most would say the folks in Stonebridge are about the friendliest around. But a dark and disturbing history is the backbone that continues to haunt citizens of this quaint town where many have secrets they never intend to reveal.

Visit www.cindystark.com for more titles and release information. Sign up for Cindy's newsletter to ensure you're always hearing the latest happenings.

PROLOGUE

Stonebridge, Massachusetts 1687

A brisk autumn breeze stirred the dried leaves around Clarabelle and her three friends as they sat in a circle, hidden from view in the deep woods. Their fathers would take a whip to them if they knew what the four fifteen-year-old witches did once they'd slipped from view. But, it was common knowledge that the power of one could be enhanced by like-minded souls if they bonded through magic.

Genevieve with her curly auburn hair glanced at each of them, her expression serious. The power of the forest burned in her bright green eyes. She leaned closer to the center of the circle although no one was around to overhear. "I overheard Mr. Bayley tell my father that his wife's distant cousin was tried and hanged in England."

Eliza, the naïve one in the group, gasped. "How horrifying. I had hoped the rumors weren't true." Clarabelle had always been jealous of Eliza's willowy figure, luxurious hair the color of wheat, and blue eyes. But, what Clarabelle lacked in the looks area, the Blessed Mother had made up for in strength and magic.

"Oh, they are true," Lily said and tossed a long, dark braid over her shoulder. "They want all witches dead. Be aware. If it is happening across the ocean, it will happen here, too."

Clarabelle narrowed her eyes at Lily's attempt to frighten Eliza. Out of all of them, Lily tended to thrive on the dramatic. Just last week, Lily had talked of a toad twice the size of her father's fist.

Clarabelle had seen that toad, too, and Lily's exaggeration was more than extreme.

"Stop," Clarabelle said. "You don't need to scare us. We understand. We have to learn stronger magic."

Genevieve and Eliza agreed with nods of their heads, which sent waves of irritation and anger rolling off Lily. Clarabelle raised the invisible shields she'd created in her mind to protect her from the emotions of others.

Lily narrowed a harsh gaze toward Clarabelle. "Mock me now, and we'll all pay for it later."

"I'm not mocking you," Clarabelle reassured. "In fact, I found my mother's spell book and memorized a truth-telling spell. Do you want to try it?"

Genevieve and Eliza looked at each other with hesitant gazes as though waiting for the other to react.

Lily nodded in approval. "Let's do it."

"Is it a blood spell?" Eliza asked, her voice innocent and sweet. If it hadn't been for Clarabelle and the other two, Eliza would have led the most boring and safe life ever.

Knowing how some of her friends would react, Clarabelle had specifically chosen one that didn't require blood, though it tended to lean toward the darker side. "No blood. It's easy and simple."

She pulled out a small container of milk, another of vinegar, and a pouch of sugar, ingredients she'd smuggled into her gathering bag before she'd left the house.

Her friends eyed the items. "Is that it?" Genevieve asked.

Clarabelle nodded and met the gazes of her three friends with a confident one of her own. "If we don't practice, we can't learn."

"Let's draw sticks to see who goes first," Lily said and quickly gathered four short twigs from the grass behind her. She curled a fist around them, evened the tops so they looked the same, and held them out to Clarabelle.

One by one, they pulled twigs and measured, leaving Eliza with the smallest. Her eyes grew wide with uncertainty.

"Don't worry," Clarabelle reassured her. "It can't hurt you."

Eliza swallowed and nodded.

Clarabelle explained the ratio of milk, vinegar and sugar as she poured the latter two into the milk container and swirled it. She set the container in the center of the them before taking Eliza's and Genevieve's hands. The other two held Lily's hands, completing the circle.

"Repeat after me. Whether truth be sweet or sour, let it pour from thy mouth this very hour. I call upon the powers that be, bring forth the truth, so mote it be."

Her friends repeated the words, and the air around Clarabelle vibrated with electricity. She lifted the container and held it out to Eliza.

Eliza hesitated for a moment and then succumbed to their peer pressure. She glanced at each of them and lifted it toward her lips. She sniffed it, met their expectant gazes, and then downed the contents.

They all froze as they waited for the spell to take effect.

"Do you feel any different?" Genevieve asked.

Eliza shook her head. "It tasted funny, but that's it."

Lily snorted. "I doubt it worked."

Clarabelle fought to tame the fire inside. "Maybe we should check before we decide." She lifted a challenging brow at Lily.

A brief smile touched Genevieve's lips, and she shifted her gaze to Eliza. "I know. Have you ever held hands with Thomas Williams?"

Touching of any kind with the opposite sex was forbidden by the church until a couple was married. But Clarabelle and her friends knew Thomas had been a long-time admirer of Eliza, and they'd often wondered if Eliza and Thomas had broken the rules.

A vivid blush darkened Eliza's cheeks, and her eyes grew wide. "Yes," she said softly, even as anger rippled from her.

Lily shot Clarabelle a grudging look of respect, fueling Clarabelle's ego. Clarabelle turned to Eliza. "Have you ever let him kiss you?" she asked in a teasing tone.

Desperation joined with Eliza's anger. "Yes," she said between gritted teeth, earning her a surprised chuckle from Lily.

"This isn't funny," Eliza complained. She got to her knees, but Lily grabbed her arm before she could stand.

"I haven't had my turn," Lily said. "Have you ever let Thomas touch you somewhere...private?" she asked sweetly.

Eliza jerked her arm free and stood. "Yes." She burst into tears and dashed off into the trees.

Clarabelle flicked her gaze between her two remaining friends. "I think we took that too far." She'd never wanted to hurt her dear friend.

Lily snorted. "Oh, please. We all must sacrifice if we want to learn. Besides, knowing what I do now, I actually think more of her."

Clarabelle, too, had been stunned by her declaration. Eliza wasn't what she seemed. Clarabelle shifted her gaze from Lily to Genevieve and wondered what secrets they might also harbor.

The sound of a gunshot ringing at a close distance brought them all to their feet, and they scattered in different directions.

To be caught gathered in the woods put them all at risk.

CHAPTER ONE

Current Day

Hazel Hardy hugged her jacket tighter around her as she hurried from her teashop along the cobblestone sidewalk of Main Street, small town Stonebridge, Massachusetts, to the cozy café down the block. The quaint town had enjoyed a very mild March, but as the month drew to a close, it seemed the Blessed Mother had changed her mind.

Ominous metal-gray clouds and a blustery wind warned of the high possibility of drenching rain. The weatherman said it would arrive some time that afternoon, which was why she'd decided to run to Cora's Café to make her delivery before the worst of the Nor'easter hit.

She neared the café door and caught a glimpse of a small sign tucked against the front window. It stated they proudly served Hazel's handcrafted teas, and she smiled. Her new partnership with Cora was working out very well. The town had accepted her as one of their own and many had gone out of their way to support her and her budding business.

If they knew the truth, that this same town had once persecuted her ancestral grandmother for being a witch, things would be much different. To this day, many of the prominent families in Stonebridge still feared and despised witches. If they discovered Hazel's identity, they'd likely run her out of town...or worse.

At least according to the police chief. And she had no reason to believe Chief Peter Parrish would exaggerate or lie.

Hazel gripped the café's doorknob and pulled, struggling to open the door against the strong winds. When she managed to get inside, the door pushed closed behind her as though warning her to take shelter and not leave until the storm had passed.

A few of the long-time residents sat in the old-fashioned eatery, enjoying the fried ham and scrambled egg special Cora always served on Tuesdays. A touch of cinnamon clung to the coffee-stained air, making her stomach growl.

"You had breakfast," she mumbled in return.

"Hazel," Cora called out from behind the counter and tucked a pencil into her blond, messy bun. Her smile was warm and welcoming as always, and it deepened the smile creases in her cheeks. By the time Cora was an old lady, the creases would likely be permanent wrinkles, but she'd be beautiful anyway.

Her friend deserted her spot behind the counter and approached. "You didn't have to come today. Not with the Witches' Wrath about to hit."

Hazel shrugged and pointed at the more-hardy citizens of Stonebridge. "If they're not worried, I'm not."

She hadn't experienced one of the town's epic storms yet, but she'd read about them in a book on the town's history that she'd borrowed from the library. Hazel wasn't sure if she believed what the author had written, but she claimed several of The Named, including Hazel's grandmother, had created the mother of all storms back in sixteen-ninety-something to punish the town during Ostara, the Spring Equinox.

The crazy storms had been happening this time of year ever since.

"The winds will knock over a few trees." The middle-aged Dotty Fingleton piped up from her seat in a nearby booth that she shared with her sister, June, and her teenaged daughter, Sophie. The family's tree had roots growing back to a wealthy ship merchant who helped settle the town. "Then it'll dump some snow and be done, Cora. Same as always. I doubt it will be a big deal."

Before Hazel had learned otherwise, she never would have guessed Dotty and June were sisters. Dotty wore her bleached blond hair piled on top of her head giving her a sexy but disheveled look, and she preferred a younger-style of clothing.

June, on the other hand, embraced her age as far as clothing went. She kept her hair dyed red and closely cropped.

Dotty's daughter, Sophie, was a spitting image of her mother, thirty years younger, and probably just as much sass as her mother had had at that age.

Cora wiggled her pointer finger in contradiction. "Not a big deal? You're forgetting that one year when we got three feet of snow and it knocked the power out. We couldn't do anything for five days."

June nodded in agreement with Cora. "She's right. We all should be tucked safe in our homes long before two o'clock when they predict the storm will make a direct hit. I know I will be."

Dotty's daughter rolled her eyes, obviously used to her mother and aunt arguing.

"Whatever happened to your adventurous spirit?" Dotty asked as she lifted her coffee cup. "You've let old age steal it from you like we promised we never would."

June snorted and waved off her dig. "Oh, go eat worms. You don't know what you're talking about."

Hazel held back her grin, still not used to the old-fashioned, quirky phrases that many of the town's residents tossed out from time to time. Chief Parrish, the nightly star in her dreams and daily pain in her butt was one of the worst offenders. She wouldn't admit it to anyone, but sometimes those silly, odd words found their way straight to her heart.

Hazel lifted the large shopping bag, boasting her teashop's logo on the front, and set it on the counter. "Four large tins of Majestic Mint and another two of spiced chai."

Cora's eyes widened in excitement. "I hope this isn't eating into the customers who come into your store for tea and a chat."

Hazel shrugged and sent her a warm smile. "Not at all. Besides, as long as they're drinking my tea, I don't care where they're getting it."

"Spoken like a true businesswoman." Cora slipped around the side of the counter and tucked the tins below it. When she straightened, she had a small brown bakery box in her hands. "I've had another idea, too."

The contents of the box piqued her interest. "What do you have there?"

"Cookies," Cora said with enthusiasm shining in her eyes. "I wondered if you'd place these complimentary cookies in your shop. I had a few of these business cards printed that you could sit next to them. I hope to attract more of the summer visitors."

Hazel glanced at the cards that stated if they visited Cora's Café and presented the card, they could get another free one to take home for later, plus ten-percent off their café bill.

"That's so smart. One taste of your chocolate chip or snickerdoodle cookies, and you know they'll be in here begging for at least a dozen more. They'll probably stay for lunch or dinner, too."

Cora beamed. "That's what I'm hoping. I really need to cash in on the tourist season to keep my bottom line out of the red. Last year's sales weren't so great."

"Really?" She'd be so sad if Cora went out of business because she couldn't make ends meet, and she vowed to eat there more often.

The sound of a loud crash coming from outside snatched their attention.

June stood so she could see out the window. "There goes Elmer's sign, tumbling down the street."

Hazel's anxiety kicked up a notch. "Hope that doesn't happen to my store."

"Me, too. But at this point, all we can do is hope for the best and ride out the storm." She gave Hazel a carefree shrug. "Besides, Elmer's sign was barely hanging up as it was."

True. As soon as she left the café, she'd ask the Blessed Mother to protect them all.

With her worries slightly eased, another idea popped into Hazel's mind. "What if you bake cookies and brownies for me to sell in my shop? We can still do the complimentary cookie, but this way might catch those who don't intend to stay long enough to eat. Also, it will allow me to live up to the temptation part of Hazel's Teas and Temptations. Packaged cookies don't create frenzied desire like your cherry macaroons."

She ought to know. She'd eaten enough of them over the past few months.

Cora drew her brows together in thought as though she was working out the logistics of it. "I think that might actually work..."

Then Cora's face brightened. "Thanks, Hazel. You're the best. Have I mentioned that I'm super glad you moved here?"

"Only a thousand times, but I don't mind. I'm glad to be here, too."

She would continue to be happy as long as no one in town learned of the witch blood flowing through her veins. If they believed Hazel was what they termed a normal person, they'd be quite content to let her stay.

She shuddered to think of what might happen if anyone found out otherwise.

"So..." Cora said, dragging out the word. "How's Peter?"

CHAPTER TWO

Hazel wanted to groan in frustration, but that might encourage Cora's interest in her so-called love life. Instead, she pasted an innocent look on her face and leaned against the café's counter. "Chief Parrish? I don't know. Did something happen to him?"

"No." Cora's gaze turned sly. "I heard you two were dating."

She snorted. "Uh, that would be a negative. We are definitely not dating."

Not that she hadn't dreamt of it, but dating the town's chief who despised witches could only end in disaster. She'd caved to her emotions and held his hand one time, and now, she couldn't forget the feel of him. Dating would only make that worse.

The front door opened and slammed shut again, bringing with it a cold whip of blustery air.

Hazel, along with everyone else in the café, turned to the stranger who'd walked through the door. He unwound the scarf from his head to reveal a middle-aged, round face. A thick layer of scruff covered his chin, and he looked like he hadn't showered or combed his hair for days.

"Welcome to Cora's Café," Cora called. "Have a seat, and I'll be with you in a minute."

He lifted his chin in appreciation and smiled as he approached the counter. "Actually, I'm not in town for long. A coffee to go would be great. Throw in a muffin if you have one."

"You're planning to drive out of town right away?" Cora shot a glance at the clock over her shoulder. "You do realize you've picked a heck of a day to visit our little town. A big storm is looming on the horizon."

One of the older men sitting at the counter swiveled his gaze around, his bright blue eyes a contrast to his sallow and wrinkled skin. "Ought to listen to the lady," he warned.

Cora smiled at the older man before returning her gaze to the stranger. "You might reconsider renting a room at the motel because you'll likely be stuck here overnight."

"I've got four-wheel drive," the stranger said, his Jersey accent strong. "I'll be fine. Besides, my business here won't take long, and then I'll be back on the road."

Cora poured coffee in a to-go container. "Trust me. Unless you're prepared to be stranded on the road for a couple of days, you should get a room. You won't regret it."

He nodded but didn't verbalize his agreement, and Hazel suspected he wasn't a man who listened to reason. "I'm looking for Dotty Fingleton. I stopped by her house, and her housekeeper said I could find her here."

Dotty rotated her frosted-blond head around until she was looking at them over the back of her booth. "I'm Dotty Fingleton. Why would you be looking for me?"

The man cleared his throat and strode forward. The card he dug from his pocket and presented to her looked like it had ridden around in his jeans for quite some time. "Arnie James. Antique dealer out of Boston. I have a client who wanted me to contact you to see if you'd be interested in selling the King's Pearls."

Dotty dropped the card on the table and brought a hand to her throat. "The pearls? How could someone even know that I have them?"

"I can't discuss the details, but I'll just say I'm very good at what I do."

"Good at accosting women in public so you can take their jewels?" Her voice had risen several octaves.

"Dotty," her sister cautioned. "Don't let him upset you. The poor man hasn't accosted you. He only asked a question."

"Yeah, Mom," Sophie added, flicking her gaze between her mother and the man. "You don't have to freak out."

Dotty focused on her sister for a long moment and then released a large exhale. "Who exactly is this client who knows about my necklace?"

The stranger snorted. "Forgive me for saying so, but the location of the pearls given to your family by King William all those years ago isn't exactly black ops intelligence." The man puffed out his chest as he inhaled. "Specialized research led me in the right direction, followed by a few well-placed phone calls."

"You didn't answer my question." Dotty's voice had regained its nervous quality. "Who is your client?"

His half-hearted attempt at an apologetic smile failed. "My client wishes to remain anonymous."

"Then you can leave." Dotty jerked her thumb over her shoulder toward the front door.

He widened his eyes as though her response surprised him. "You haven't even heard my offer yet. Come on. It's five figures."

She eyed him with a cold stare. "I don't care what you're offering. Those pearls have been in my family for hundreds of years, and they will continue to stay that way. When I die, they will go to my daughter and then her daughter."

Sophie smiled smugly.

"Why?" His question held a whining quality. "You probably have them buried in a safe where no one ever sees them. What good are they there? Passed down from generation to generation like a burden that must be carried because the one before you did the same. Why don't you sell them to someone who really wants them? Someone who will take pleasure from them every day? You can take the money and buy yourself something nice."

Dotty snorted in disbelief. "Cora? Do you have this man's coffee and muffin ready? Because he's leaving."

Cora flicked a wide-eyed glance at Hazel, and she returned the gesture. "Coming right up."

The disappointed man headed toward the counter and paid for his food, but he stopped at their table again before leaving. "Call me if you change your mind."

Dotty turned her face from him. "Rest assured. I won't."

For several moments after the man had exited, no one in the café said a word.

Finally, Dotty released an exaggerated huff. "The nerve of some people."

"Right?" Sophie added. "Like he can just waltz in and take my inheritance from me?"

June shook her head. "I think you made a big deal out of nothing. He was only asking a question."

Just like that, the sisters were arguing again.

Cora watched them for a few seconds before turning her gaze to Hazel. "Nothing much changes around here."

Hazel grinned. "One of the things I love about Stonebridge."

Not long after, Hazel said her goodbyes, and she left with a package of Cora's amazing snickerdoodles and chocolate chip cookies tucked safely under her arm. As she forced open the door and stepped out, she smiled. She might be in for a heck of a storm, but she'd have no one in her store to eat the cookies.

She'd told Gretta to stay home, knowing business would be light and they'd be closing early, so Hazel wouldn't even have her assistant to help her devour them.

The Blessed Mother knew she wouldn't waste something so delicious.

If she couldn't eat them all, which was unlikely, she could freeze them for later.

She lowered her head against the blowing snow and headed down the cobblestone sidewalk toward her shop.

Several steps later, she barreled straight into a hard body.

CHAPTER THREE

Instead of flying backward from the impact, strong arms wrapped around Hazel and held her steady. She lifted her gaze, not at all surprised at who she'd literally run into.

"Whoa, there." Police Chief Peter Parrish chuckled as she stared into his engaging green eyes and cursed her luck. He was as tempting and as bad for her as Cora's cookies.

Her heartbeat danced to a crazy tune as she stepped back, creating a safe distance between them. She recalled they'd had a similar incident once at the grocery store and narrowed her eyes. "You did that on purpose."

"Did not," he countered. "A snowflake fluttered into my eye, and I was blinking when *you* crashed into *me*. If I'd been a light pole, you'd be splayed on the sidewalk with splitting headache."

A man in uniform always caught her attention, but Peter was no ordinary officer. He exuded confidence and charisma. The brilliant mind behind those sexy eyes might be more attractive to her than the muscled package he came in. "Of course, you had lightning quick reflexes to catch me before I fell." All in all, he was as dangerous as they came. At least to her.

He shrugged, his smile warming every inch of her. "What can I say? It's one of my many fine traits."

She nodded, trying to glare, but failed to keep a smile from her lips. "I'm sure."

"Hey." He turned and faced the direction she'd been walking. "You know a big storm is coming. You should be inside where you're safe, so I don't have to worry."

She gave him a sideways glance and fluttered her lashes. "You would worry about me?"

"Stop that," he warned, his teasing laced with a hint of seriousness. "You know I do."

She did, in fact, know that very thing.

As much as she tried to ignore whatever was blossoming between them, or hide it from everyone around them when she couldn't manage that, Peter had been clear he was in pursuit of her. She'd been the one to hold him back, to keep him at a safe distance that wouldn't endanger her heart, and therefore endanger her life.

Unfortunately, she sort of sucked at it.

She exhaled and shook her head in fake exasperation, acknowledging that she did know he cared without having to speak it. Then she began to walk toward her shop. "Don't worry. I'm headed back to work right now."

He followed, of course. "I meant safe inside your home. Not your shop."

She glanced about the deserted street. At least there wouldn't be many out today who would see them and add fuel to the gossip already circulating around town about the two of them. Heck, rumors of their once non-existent relationship had begun before there was anything to talk about. In a town that small, it didn't matter. If there wasn't an interesting story to spread, people made up stuff.

Which was quite possibly how her many-times-over, great grandmother had ended up at the bottom of a lake with her pockets stuffed with stones more than three hundred years ago. The town's historic rumors were much worse than the current ones embellishing her love life.

Hazel had tried many times to imagine and empathize with the horrors Clarabelle must have endured, but she still found it hard to conceive that residents of a quiet, pretty town such as Stonebridge could turn that vicious.

She shook off her oppressive thoughts. "I need to do a few things first, and then I'll go home," she told Peter. "I promise to leave well before the storm hits."

"Okay."

She stopped in front of her store and turned to him. "Okay, what?"

"Okay, I'll wait."

Her pulse kicked into a higher gear, and she lifted her keys and unlocked her shop. "I don't need you to wait. I'm a big girl, capable of finding my way home."

He pushed open the door for her. "I know. It's for my sake, not yours."

He indicated she should enter, and when she did, he followed her inside. He inhaled deeply. "It always smells so good in here."

Tiny bubbles of happiness erupted inside her. "Thank you."

He rubbed his hands together and blew into them. "It's really cold out there. I don't suppose you have water heated for tea."

She rolled her eyes but smiled. "Hot water in the pot. You know where it is."

"But I like it better when you make it." He grinned.

"I need to finish up so I can get home before the storm. If you want some, you're on your own today." She thrust the box of cookies until it bumped his chest. "Take these, too." She knew she'd regret it later, but it was for the best.

"What are they?" He lifted the lid. "Oh, dang. From Cora's?"

"Mmm-hmm..." She headed into the backroom to put away the herbs she'd been working with earlier. She stuffed lavender into a bag and sealed it and then covered the canister of imported Asian black tea.

She placed both on a shelf, turned, and let out a squeal of surprise when she found Peter standing a short distance away. "Did you have to scare me like that?"

He held a half-eaten chocolate chip cookie in his hand and a smile on his face as he chewed and then swallowed. "I'd say I'm sorry, but you wouldn't believe me."

"You've got that right." She swept the remnants of her work from that morning into a little trash can and then headed toward him.

When he didn't move out of the doorway so she could pass, she looked up at him expectantly.

"You should let me watch you work one day. This room is fascinating. I'd like to see what you do with everything. How you come up with ideas for teas that make them taste good."

No good witch worth her cauldron let anyone but the most trusted individuals watch her work. She might want to trust Peter, but she knew in her heart she couldn't. "Uh...no." She shook her head.

"Why not? Are you afraid I'll see you cast a spell or something?"

Her insides froze, and she pushed against his chest, forcing him to move. "Funny." Except he'd hit the nail right on the head.

She gathered invoices and tucked them into a drawer. "How many of these storms have you weathered? Are they really that bad?"

"As long as I can remember except for the few years I'd moved away from Stonebridge. Trust me, they can be brutal."

"So, you grew up here?"

"Yep."

Which meant he'd had a lifetime of brainwashing by the town who feared her kind.

"Loved playing in the river and riding my bike wherever I wanted. I'd hoped to raise my kids here."

And he wanted kids. Or at least he had with his previous wife. She highly doubted he'd want witch blood in those children.

Too many instances had showed her repeatedly that, as much as her energy blended well with his, he wasn't the man for her.

She turned off the teapot, took a quick glance around, and then focused on him, forcing a smile. "I think that's it. Everything's put away. I just need to turn off the lights."

"Don't forget the cookies."

She snorted, happy to embrace something besides her fears. "Let me sneak a snickerdoodle, and then why don't you take the rest to the station? I'm sure everyone who's working during the next twelve hours will appreciate them."

She hated to let them go, but if she took them home, she knew she'd eat every single one of them. He handed one to her, and she wrapped it in a napkin and tucked it in her purse.

Peter stopped at the front door while she turned off the lights, and then she faced him. They stood only inches apart, and though the storm had begun to rage outside, her little corner of the world was quite cozy. "Ready?"

He stared at her for a long moment. "When are you going to let me take you to dinner?"

She chuckled at his tenacity and shook her head. "Never."

"You let me hold your hand in the woods."

Which had been the first step down a slippery slope. "I shouldn't have."

"It was nice," he countered.

She sighed. She couldn't argue with that. "I should get home."

"Okay, but like it or not, I'm seeing you safely there."

"Fine." Even if she said no, he'd follow her.

The walk to her house was short but cold and snowy. Peter didn't stick around after she unlocked her door since he needed to be at the station, but he made Hazel promise she'd call if she needed anything. So, she promised even if she didn't mean it.

As Peter headed back toward Main Street, a flash of burnt orange streaked across the road in front of her house and darted beneath her car. She squinted, trying to see better through the thickly falling snow. She gasped. It looked like the cat who'd hung around Clarabelle's old home. But that couldn't be.

If it was, that meant he would have traveled clear across town to find her, and she couldn't fathom why he would be at her house when he had a perfectly good place to hunker down for the storm. She knew for a fact he could get in and out of that house.

She waited until Peter was far enough away that he couldn't hear her. "Here, kitty-kitty," she called. Regardless of whether or not it was the same crazed animal, she couldn't leave the poor thing out in the cold. She'd survive sheltering with it for a few days.

A few seconds later, familiar green eyes and a pink nose peeked from beneath the car.

No. It couldn't be. But it was.

She was surprised, and yet, she wasn't.

"What are you doing here?" she hissed. "Did you follow me home?"

The thought that he might be stalking her left her uneasy.

The sassy cat released a long, multi-toned yowl that seemed an awful lot like it was berating her.

She shook her head in frustration. "I don't understand a word...er, a meow of what you said."

The cat repeated the caterwaul.

"Say it however many times you like. I'm still not going to understand."

Let me in.

A disembodied voice whispered through the wintry air.

Or was it a feeling and not actual words? Voices in her head?

Second thoughts of leaving the cat out in the cold crossed her mind now that she knew it was him. The last time they'd been alone together, he'd caused her to fall down the stairs.

And find the ancient book of spells.

As though that made everything okay.

She glared at him for a few moments as frosty air froze her nose. Then she groaned. "Fine. Get in here."

The cat dashed from beneath the car and between her legs into the house. She closed the door, locking out the storm, and turned. The sly cat had vanished.

"This should be fun," she grumbled as she set off to find him. They'd likely endure days of torture before either of them could leave.

CHAPTER FOUR

Cora's prediction of a two-day white out was spot on. Hazel had stayed snug in her little house, keeping an eye out for the mysterious cat who mostly remained in hiding.

Howling winds had accompanied massive amounts of snow. All activities in Stonebridge had screeched to a halt while the town paid its yearly penance for drowning witches all those years ago. As an earth witch, she knew storms and the damage they brought were a necessary part of nature, but she'd never liked the screeching of the trees as they battled the elements. This time was no different.

She hoped Peter and his officers had stayed warm.

Funny how legends and lore built over time, becoming interesting stories to tell kids and tourists, but little truth likely remained.

She preferred to believe the town suffered a nasty storm the winter after they'd committed their vicious deeds. And like residents were still wont to do, they blamed everything that went wrong on the poor witches who'd been unlucky enough to choose Stonebridge as a home, including her long-ago grandmother, Clarabelle Foster Hardy.

The entity she'd encountered at Clarabelle's house, whom she believed to be her ancestor, hadn't exuded a cruel vibe. Hazel had only experience warmth and welcome. Yes, there were darker spells toward the back of Clarabelle's book, but she was sure those had been for protection only.

On day three, the sun came out and brightened Hazel's mood considerably. She was relieved to find her house hadn't sustained damage. The worst she'd incurred was several downed tree limbs.

She itched to get to the teashop to ensure all was well. If she could navigate the roads, she had daily deliveries to do, too. She had warm boots and her shop wasn't far, so she could walk this morning, and then return later to get her car if the town had cleared the streets of snow.

Boots on and bundled, she stepped out into a world of pure white. Brilliant energy bounced off at least two-feet of snowy powder and left her giddy inside. If she was a kid, she'd be all about snowmen and snowball fights.

The morning at her shop was slow, but by afternoon when Gretta arrived to start her shift, people had emerged from hiding, grateful to be out and about. Hazel left Gretta in charge of the shop and headed out for deliveries.

Instead of navigating Dotty Fingleton's hilly driveway where she might slide in her car whilst trying to maneuver, Hazel parked along the street and walked the slope instead. Several sets of footprints going both directions told her that others had chosen the same precautions.

Hazel rang the doorbell and stomped snow off her feet while she waited. A few moments later, the door opened and Dotty greeted her with a surprised but happy smile.

"Oh, my goodness, Hazel. I didn't expect you to deliver today. Not that I'm complaining. Drank the last of my teas trying to stay warm the past couple of days."

Hazel waved off her concern. "I'm happy to be out. Two days locked up alone in a house can be mighty boring, especially with no power." And a crazy cat stalking her.

She needed to remember to stop by the grocery store for cat food before she went home for the day, too. She didn't know what the rascal usually ate, but if he thought he was bringing a mouse into her house, he'd soon learn otherwise.

Dotty leaned closer to Hazel. "Agreed. My daughter is driving me insane. She drained the battery on her cell phone the first day, and she's beside herself. In my day, we kept plenty busy without being plugged in all the time. If you ask me, God would say it's not good for the soul."

Hazel had no doubt he would agree, along with the Blessed Mother.

Dotty stepped back. "Come on in while I grab your money."

She glanced downward, hating to track snow in Dotty's house. "My feet are wet."

"Between you, my daughter, and the housekeeper, I've had plenty of people in and out today. A little more snow isn't going to hurt. The farmer's son, Basil, even stopped by with fresh milk and eggs. I guess everyone is a little stir crazy. Especially with no TV or internet access." She winked and motioned Hazel inside and shut the door behind her.

The contrast in light between outdoors and inside her home was stark, and Hazel blinked, as her vision worked to adjust.

"I'll be right back," Dotty said.

She ascended the steep stairs in the old house, each one creaking as she did. Some might consider it a flaw that needed to be fixed, but Hazel preferred to think of it as proof that the house had been well-used and loved over the years. A newer home might not have those same issues, but it wouldn't have the charm, either.

A dreadful scream ripped through the house and pierced Hazel's heart.

Startled, she froze for a second and then ran for the stairs, toward Dotty's cry. Hazel took the steps two at a time and met a white-faced Dotty in the hallway.

Her daughter came running from another upstairs room. "Mom? What happened?" she asked, her voice frantic.

"Call the police," Dotty cried. "I've been robbed."

Hazel fought for a decent breath. "Robbed?"

Dotty's face crumpled in anguish. "Someone has stolen my mother's pearls."

"*What? No!*" Sophie cried. "Who would do that? Those were supposed to be mine."

Hazel's heart pounded as she slipped her phone from her pocket and dialed the emergency number. Peter's administrative assistant answered.

"Margaret. This is Hazel. I'm at Dotty Fingleton's house. Is there anyone you can send right over? She's been robbed. A valuable pearl necklace."

Margaret's response drew a shiver from her. Hazel shifted her gaze to Dotty. "Could the thief still be in the house?" she asked the two shaken women in a hushed tone.

Dotty glanced about in fright. "I don't think so, but I really don't know."

Sophie gripped her mother's arm. "What if he's still here?"

"Just send someone fast." Hazel pocketed her phone. "An officer is on his way. I suggest we wait by the front door, just in case someone is still in the house. We don't want to confront anyone."

"*Mom,*" Sophie whined, her eyes wide in fear.

Her mother wrapped an arm around her. "Let's go downstairs."

Together, the three of them waited in the foyer as seconds schlepped by like a snail.

When a siren wailed in the distance, all of them visibly relaxed. "It's going to be okay," Hazel said.

She opened the door to allow the officer entry and caught her breath when she found Peter had been the one to respond. "Chief Parrish, thank you for coming so fast."

The handsome officer didn't have his smile on today. Something primal and protective had replaced his flirting, and yet made him even more attractive. "I want the three of you to wait on the porch until I give the all clear. Do you understand?"

"It's cold out there," Sophie said.

"Do you have a coat?" Chief Parrish eyed the coat rack next to the door and then indicated with a nod that he expected them to comply.

He focused on Dotty. "Where did you keep the jewelry that was stolen?"

"My bedroom," Dotty responded with a shaky voice. "First room on the right. The safe is in my closet."

He pulled the gun from his holster, which sent a fierce shiver racing through Hazel. "Stay outside. Another unit is on the way."

If Hazel wasn't so scared, she'd take a moment to appreciate the fine picture of a fearless man willing to put himself in danger to protect them. "Let's go," she said instead and pulled the door closed behind them.

CHAPTER FIVE

Chief Parrish and another officer cleared the house and allowed them re-entry within ten minutes, directing them into the ornately decorated sitting room, complete with Tiffany lamps and antique tables.

"Whoever took the pearls is long gone," Peter said. "I'd like the three of you to sit down with me, and let's go over what we know."

"We don't know anything." Dotty's voice rose with hysteria. "They are my mother's priceless jewels. The pearls given to my family by King William the Third several hundred years ago. This morning they were here, and now, they're gone."

Chief Parrish lifted a calming hand. "I know. They are very precious and valuable, but the more I can learn, things that you might not think are important, the more likely I'll be able to find your pearls and the person who committed the crime. Do you need a minute, or can we start now?"

Tears wetted Dotty's cheeks, and she waved a frenzied hand in front of her face. "I need a minute."

"It's okay," the chief said. "This is normal behavior for someone who has suffered a shock."

"I'll help you, Mom." Sophie stood and took her mother's hand. "Some cold water on your face might help."

"Yes, yes." Dotty wrapped her fingers around her daughter's elbow, and Sophie led her away.

When they'd exited the room, Peter turned to Hazel. "How did you end up in the middle of this?"

She widened her eyes in innocence. "It's not my fault. I was here to make a delivery. Dotty went to retrieve money and then screamed."

He released a heavy sigh and shook his head. "I guess at least no one is dead this time."

She shot a narrow-eyed glare at him. "What is that supposed to mean?"

He pinned her with a direct gaze. "It means you attract trouble, and that doesn't sit well with me."

Where was the fun and interesting guy who appreciated her help on cases?

She folded her arms. "You think it sits well with me?"

Sounds in the hallway brought their private conversation to a halt.

Dotty sniffed as she found a seat on the vintage, red velvet couch. "I think I can answer your questions now."

Peter's gaze lost its fire and grew kind before he addressed Dotty. "When did you first notice the pearls were missing?"

"I told you already," Hazel responded.

The chief flicked a warning glance in her direction. "Let Dotty answer please."

She growled inside. At times, the man was not worth the bother.

"Hazel brought my tea, and I went upstairs for my purse. That's when I saw the safe part-way open. I looked inside, and they were gone." Tears welled in her eyes again.

"When was the last time you knew for sure the safe was closed?"

Dotty frowned. "Last night, I suppose."

Peter tilted his head. "You suppose, or you know?"

She shook her hands in frustration. "I don't know. It's always closed. That's why I noticed today when it wasn't."

The chief jotted notes on a small pad. "When was the last time you accessed it?"

"I...I don't know. A month ago?" The poor woman's anguish rolled off her in waves, causing knots in Hazel's stomach.

"It was Grandma's birthday," Sophie said. "Auntie June was over, and you were remembering what it was like when Grandma was alive. Auntie June asked to wear the pearls at dinner. For fun, since she never gets a chance, remember?"

"That's right." Dotty nodded in relief. "I know for certain I put them back after June left for the night."

Peter nodded as he wrote. "And you shut and locked it for sure?"

Dotty sighed and closed her eyes in defeat. "I think so, but I don't know."

Sophie took her mom's hand, gave her a sympathetic look, and then focused on the chief. "Mom closes it but doesn't lock it because she can't remember the combination, and she doesn't want to get it from downstairs."

Dotty's expression fell. "This is all my fault. How could I have been so careless with something so precious?"

Sophie slid a sideways glance at her mother. Hazel sensed the girl sympathized with her mom, but anger was mixed in with her emotions, too. "It's okay, Mom. They'll find the thief. With all this snow, whoever did it can't get very far."

Dotty turned her red-rimmed watery gaze to her daughter. "What if they don't find them? Then what?"

The expression on Sophie's face grew angry. "They have to. Those pearls were supposed to be mine."

"Mom?" A male voice from the doorway stole Hazel's attention. A lanky, twenty-something young man with dishwater blond hair stood at the entrance with a concerned look. "What's going on? Is everything okay?"

Dotty's deep inhale ended in a sob, and she held out her hand to the man Hazel assumed was her son. "Oh, Scott," her voice cracked when she said his name. "Someone broke in and took the family pearls."

"*Seriously?*" Pulses of anger colored his words red. He strode forward and grasped his mother's hand. One by one, he glanced at each face in the room, stopping on his sister. "Are you sure you didn't take them, Sophie?"

Sophie's mouth fell open as hatred lit her expression. "*You're a pig, Scott.* Why would I take them? That's like stealing from myself." She pointed a finger at him. "More likely you did. You can't stand that I get them and you don't."

Loathing emanated from the son. "Why *should* you get them just because you're a girl? I'm the oldest."

"You wouldn't wear them," Sophie countered.

"Mom doesn't either," he shot back.

"Enough!" Dotty raised her hands as though they were white flags. "Bickering isn't going to help us find them. Both of you need to leave. I can't stand you right now."

The siblings glared at each other for several long seconds, and then Sophie turned and headed out of the room first. Scott followed closely behind her, and Hazel couldn't help but think their arguing wasn't over.

"Don't leave the house," the chief called after them. "I'll need to question both of you, too."

Scott paused outside the doorway. "I don't know anything. I just got here."

Chief Parrish stood and faced the kid. "All the same, stick around. Don't leave the house until we've talked."

"Whatever," Scott answered, backing down. "I'll be in my room."

Hazel, Peter, and Dotty all remained quiet until her children's footsteps faded. "Scott's been away at school, right?" he asked Dotty.

She nodded. "This is his second year at Utica College."

"Does he usually come home for the weekends?" Peter resumed his seat. "That's quite a drive."

"No." Dotty dabbed at her eyes. "This is the first time this semester. I wasn't expecting him until May. Maybe it's the mid-semester break."

Peter muttered an unintelligible word as he took notes. Then he glanced up. "Who has been in the house this morning besides your children and us?"

"My cleaning lady Emma Jones. She walked over early since she doesn't live far. She took out the trash and cleaned some, and then headed to the grocery store for me."

Chief Parrish scrawled more notes. "Anyone else?"

"No," Dotty said.

"Wait," Hazel interrupted. "Didn't you say Basil had stopped by, too, with fresh milk and eggs?"

Hazel hadn't met the kid and therefore didn't know if he was the type to steal. But at this point, they couldn't rule out anyone.

"Yes." Dotty nodded fervently and then slowed. "But he was only in the house for a moment. I let him in and sent him back to the kitchen, and then I went back to..."

Dotty's expression crumpled. "I returned to the study to read. He knows his way out. We follow this routine all the time."

"But you don't know for a fact the exact time he left the house?" the chief asked.

"No," Dotty answered softly. "I do not. I suppose if he knew what he was doing, he could have slipped upstairs. But, I can't see Basil taking them. Other than spending too much time looking at my Sophie, he's a good boy."

Chief Parrish shrugged. "We don't always know people as well as we think. Sometimes, they aren't at all who we think they are." He flicked a glance at Hazel, and she froze.

Had he directed that comment at her, or was his glance coincidental?

Either way, Hazel's nerves fidgeted. "Chief, I need to finish my deliveries for the morning, and I really don't have much to add. I was only here long enough to hear Dotty scream and call for help. Is it okay if I get going?"

Peter gave her a quick nod. "As long as you stop by the station later and give me an official statement."

Out of the cauldron and into the fire. "No problem." She stood and gave Dotty a hug. "Call me if I can help with anything."

Dotty patted her hand. "Thank you, love. I'm so glad you arrived when you did."

"Of course." Hazel caught Peter's gaze and pretended she didn't feel the sizzle from it. "Later."

"Today?" he pressed.

"Yes." She left them with a smile even though her thoughts tumbled a million miles an hour. Who could have done such a thing?

For a town filled with a long history of pious people, they weren't as perfect as they liked to believe.

CHAPTER SIX

Hazel stepped from the porch of the Fingleton home, taking a moment to allow her eyes to adjust to the brilliant glare from the sun bouncing off the snow. She blinked a few times to clear the water from her eyes and set off along the sidewalk in front of the house.

Muted voices reached out to her, and she slowed her steps.

A male and a female...arguing?

Dotty's daughter?

Hazel picked up her pace, concerned because of what had just transpired inside.

"*No,*" the man said, sounding angry but firm.

Hazel reached the corner and stopped short to keep from colliding with a tall, muscled, red-headed young man.

He gave her a quick glance, his face red and jaw clenched, and then continued, striding down the driveway toward an old rusty gray truck that had been parked not far from her car.

Sophie released a sob, and Hazel swung around to face her. The poor girl had tears streaming down her face and struggled to breathe.

"Sophie? Are you okay? What did he do?"

She shook her head, not giving an answer.

"Who was that? Did he hurt you?" Hazel pressed.

"No." Sophie's features grew more distressed as she watched the young man drive away. She blinked rapidly and then met Hazel's gaze. "I...I shouldn't have asked, but I needed to know. Now, he hates me."

"Asked what?" The girl made no sense. "Who was he?"

"Basil. I asked if he knew anything about my mother's pearls, and he got angry, said I was accusing him. I wasn't. I just...I needed to know."

So, that was Basil. "I thought he'd left earlier. Why'd he come back?"

"I asked him to because I wanted to see his face. But, I was so stupid. He's a good guy who wouldn't hurt anyone ever." She sniffed and glanced again in the direction he'd gone. "I should go inside. My mom and the chief will be looking for me."

"Of course. Do let them know what happened with Basil. It might save some heartache later."

Sophie nodded and then hurried around the back of the house to the door she must have used to leave in the first place.

Hazel frowned as she watched her go. At least she'd have something to report to Peter when she saw him later, and her visit wouldn't be a complete waste of time.

Oh, who was she kidding? She loved that he was attracted to her and hated herself for loving it. Seeing him would never be a waste of her time.

Not that she'd admit that aloud.

She sighed as she made her way down the slippery driveway, cursing her crazy feelings. Not only was she a witch, but her mind was a very messed up place to be.

If Peter was smart, he'd run in the other direction.

CHAPTER SEVEN

Hazel waited until after her teashop closed for the day before she drew up her collar and walked the short distance to the police station. This way, she didn't have to explain to Gretta where she was going and why. Her assistant was a smart woman, and she already had her suspicions about Hazel and Peter's flirtations, which Hazel had vehemently denied.

No sense giving her more fodder for her wild stories.

By the time she reached the old courthouse that housed the police station, the frosty air had chilled her nose and toes. She never tired of viewing the charming old building built more than a hundred years ago from gray stones of various sizes held together by plenty of mortar. Her ancestral heritage first brought Stonebridge to her attention, but the historical architecture encouraged her to visit the town, which led to her wanting to stay. That and the fact her ex didn't live here.

The downside to waiting until her shop had closed meant that the receptionist Margaret had already left the police station for the day. As far as Hazel could tell, only one other officer remained in the office, seated at the far end of the room, and he had his attention glued to a computer screen. She walked toward Peter's office, half-hoping he might be out as well.

She peeked inside and found him at his desk, also fixated on a computer screen. His gaze flicked from his work to her in an instant, and then a smile broke over his face that left her knees weak. "Hazel. Come in."

He stood and helped her with her coat, and then proceeded to shut the door, closing off the outside world. "I thought you'd forgotten."

She claimed her usual seat. "Sorry it took me so long. The shop was kind of busy this afternoon."

He slid behind his desk and focused on her eyes. Then smiled. "You do realize you're a terrible liar, right?"

She lifted her brows in an innocent gesture as her throat tightened. "What do you mean?"

"Really? Was your shop that busy? Or were you waiting until most people in town had gone home so you wouldn't be seen with me once again?" The man was too smart for his own good.

She pursed her lips. "There's nothing wrong with wanting to keep gossip to a minimum. The more often I have to explain there's nothing between us, the less likely people will believe me."

He genuinely seemed confused by her explanation. "So? You're single. I'm single."

"The whole town thinks we're dating."

"Maybe we should be."

She inhaled, prepared to explain why that would be a bad idea, but he wouldn't understand without full details. And those, she couldn't give. "Maybe...you should complete your questioning so I can get home. Apparently, I'm the new owner of a cat, and I need to check on him. He wanted shelter during the storm and hasn't left yet."

He chuckled. "Did you feed it?"

"Of course, I fed him."

"Then he's officially yours. What did you name him?"

She paused for a long moment. "Kitty."

"You named your cat, Kitty?"

"Mr. Kitty?" She shrugged. "I haven't picked out a proper name yet, okay? He's salty like someone else I know, and all the names that come to mind would probably offend others."

He laughed and let it fade into a smile. "What am I going to do with you?"

She lifted her brows. "Question me about the theft at the Fingleton house?" she asked innocently.

The growl of his stomach echoed in the quiet office. "Can we order in burgers and fries while I do? I'm starving, and John will go pick them up if I buy him one, too. Can your kitty wait that long?"

She couldn't very well say no and still respect herself as a caring person. "Fine."

He grinned. "Be right back."

Less than a minute later, he was. "Great. Let's get business out of the way first, and then we can relax while we eat."

He pulled out a familiar yellow pad. "Tell me what you know."

She sighed. "This is ridiculous, you know. I don't know anything. As I said earlier, I brought my delivery. Dotty invited me inside. I waited while she ran upstairs to grab money, and then she screamed. When I got to the top of the stairs, she was in the hallway and said she'd been robbed. I called the police, and you came. The rest, you know."

"Only Sophie and Dotty in the house when you were there?"

She drew a strand of hair across her lips as she thought, trying to remember any minor details that might appease him. "As far as I know. There was one thing that happened after I left, though."

He raised his brows. "Go on."

"When I walked out of the house, I heard voices, and they didn't sound happy. I couldn't make out words...but the tone wasn't a good one. As I neared the corner, I heard a man say 'no' very firmly. It was Basil Taylor talking with Sophie. He nearly knocked me over as he was leaving."

"Did he run because he saw you?"

"No. He'd already turned and seemed as surprised to see me as I was to see him. He was angry, though. Red-faced and unhappy. Sophie was crying. After the robbery and with him being a possible suspect, I worried he'd hurt her. But she said she was upset about the pearls. She'd asked him if he knew anything, which made him angry."

Peter paused while he wrote and then focused on her again, his green eyes sparking fires inside her. "Did he seem guilty to you?"

She sighed. "Not that I could tell, but I couldn't say for sure. I told Sophie to mention the incident to you and her mom, but it sounds like she didn't."

He rolled his eyes in exasperation. "No. She bawled through most of my interview with her. I think the shock of what had happened finally hit her. Sometimes it takes a while before people realize the extent of emotional damage that happens when their supposedly-safe space is invaded."

Poor girl. "I can only imagine. I hope she's doing better tonight."

"Dotty's son is home, so I think that's helped the ladies feel safer. He has a gun, though I'm not sure that's a good thing."

Something in his tone caught her attention. "You don't trust Scott with a gun?"

Peter blew out a breath and rubbed the scruff on his chin. "Let's just say the boy wasn't always the best bun in the basket, and I think he's the type who'd shoot first and ask questions later, regardless of who walked through the door."

She snorted. "Best bun in the basket? Where do you come up with these sayings?"

He shrugged and leaned back from the desk. "Everyone says it."

"No," she said and chuckled. "Not everyone. Maybe people in Stonebridge, but I've never heard that before in my life."

"Then apparently you need to get out more."

She turned her lips into a coy smile. "Or maybe you do."

John popped his head in the door. "Food's here. Get it while it's hot."

"Let's eat," he said to Hazel and stood. She did the same and followed John into a conference room where the three of them sat down together.

Hazel had to admit she had a pleasant time. She hadn't had a chance to get to know John or his wife, Susan, but she discovered he was also a transplant to Stonebridge and was interested in the history of the town. He promised to share some of the more fascinating things he'd learned with her later.

After dinner and questioning, Peter announced he wouldn't let Hazel walk home alone in the dark. A sly smirk crossed John's lips, and she knew he'd heard the gossip as well.

She argued she'd be fine.

Peter insisted.

So, they bundled up and left.

Hazel worked to keep the conversation light as they walked side-by-side down a deserted side street. Most people had gone home for the day, leaving their world still and silent except for the sound of their shoes hitting the ground.

She made Peter wait outside while she hurried into the grocery store for cat food, but he took the bag from her the second she exited the building. He both pleased and irritated her at the same time.

When they were halfway to her house, she sensed a shift in the energy sparking between them, and she lifted her gaze to find him watching her.

"Are you going to let me hold your hand again?" he asked, taking their companionable conversation straight to heart-pounding craziness.

"No." She followed her rejection with a teasing grin.

"One of these days, Hazel, you're going to be asking me instead."

She couldn't deny that she might, so she changed the subject. "I hope you noticed the look on your officer's face when you said you were walking me home. The knowing smirk," she added when he pretended innocence.

"Didn't see it."

She knew very well he had. "Who's the bad liar now?"

"Is that your cat?"

His question caught her off guard, and she turned her gaze toward her house down the block. Sure enough, a ball of orange fur waited on the porch next to the front door.

"How in the world did he get out?" She knew for a fact he'd been inside when she'd left that morning because she'd caught him sneaking pieces of chicken from the plate she'd placed on the floor for him.

"You must have let him out."

As skittish as the cat was when she'd first encountered him, she was sure he'd run when she and Peter neared.

But, no.

Instead, Mr. Kitty watched her with a perturbed look and let Peter pet him as she unlocked the door and opened it. As soon as there was room, the cat pushed his way inside, squawking as he did.

Peter chuckled at his antics. "Sounds like you're in trouble."

She held up her hands and shot a confused look at Peter. "I know, right? I'm certain the cat hates me, but he won't leave. I can't figure him out."

"Maybe he doesn't want people to know he likes you." He leaned in and surprised her with a kiss on the cheek. "Goodnight, Miss Hardy. Sleep well."

He wore a grin as he turned and strode away.

She stepped inside, exhaled a breath of frustration, and shut the door. It seemed she now had two men in her life that enjoyed torturing her.

The spot on her cheek where Peter had placed his lips still sizzled. She closed her eyes for a moment and touched her skin. Having him hold her hand had been nice, but this was much, much nicer. She wondered what it would feel like to kiss him on the lips.

She opened her eyes and found the cat watching her with a knowing look. "What? He's the one who kissed me."

Mr. Kitty yowled, and she realized he was waiting for her to open the bag of cat food and serve him dinner.

She shook her head in defeat. "All right. All right," she grumbled as she made her way into the kitchen to find a bowl for his food.

One day, she'd pack up and leave Stonebridge, and then Peter and Mr. Kitty would both feel bad because they'd mistreated her.

CHAPTER EIGHT

Hazel stayed as far away from the police station as she could for the next couple of days, even took the long way around on a spontaneous bicycle ride before heading to town for breakfast.

It wasn't that she didn't want to see Peter. Problem was, she did. A lot. And that left her vulnerable and in danger.

She'd prayed to the Blessed Mother morning and night that her attraction might ease, but then she'd think of Peter all day or dream of him each night.

Distance was her only chance for survival.

If she thought for a minute Peter might understand or be open to her heritage, things might be different. But he'd made it clear from the very beginning what he thought of witches. His point of view had been predetermined by his ancestors long ago and passed down through the ages like a legacy.

Just like hers had.

Blood that ran that deep didn't change.

Today, she'd decided to try a different tactic and fill her mind with as many other things as possible. She'd start the warm, sunny day by celebrating Clarabelle's three hundred and forty-eighth birthday. Her morning began with a special gratitude ritual that she dedicated to her ancestral grandmother and her bravery for continuing her spiritual practice despite what others believed and despite the ultimate personal cost of doing so.

If not for Clarabelle's life, then Hazel would not be alive to enjoy the beautiful town her family had once lived in. She could also be grateful that they no longer hunted down and drowned witches like they once had.

Or did they? Peter had mentioned that anyone outwardly claiming to be a witch might disappear.

She reminded herself that she wasn't thinking about that or Peter today.

The scent of coffee and bacon reached out to her as she approached Cora's.

Food.

She would think about eating instead, and she could be guaranteed that many of her neighbors would keep her company on this fine Saturday morning.

She pulled the café doors open and a cacophony of noise and a sea of faces greeted her. Perhaps too many of her neighbors.

Her stomach growled and urged her forward. Cora passed, her arms laden with six plates of food. "Find a seat wherever. One of us will get with you when we can."

If she knew anything at all about food service, Hazel would have strapped on an apron and helped. But customers didn't want mixed up orders, and the other waitresses wouldn't want her underfoot.

She waved at many friends and searched for a table as she wound her way toward the counter where several old timers sat in flannel shirts shooting the breeze over coffee. Just beyond them, she spotted a vacant table for two. Sweet, old Mr. Fletcher grinned at her as she passed, but she was afraid if she stopped to talk, she wouldn't be able to snag the table before someone else did.

She sat and nodded to John who stood at the counter, who was likely getting food for the guys at the police station, hopefully including Peter.

One of Cora's waitresses, Belinda, set a coffee mug on her table and filled it. "What can I get you?" Her brilliant blue eyes, accentuated by black, cat-eye liner, held traces of impatience.

Belinda always seemed to be full of herself, constantly checking her appearance in the mirror behind the counter, as though that was all that mattered in the world. One day, when her looks were gone, maybe she'd discover there was more to life.

"The special is fine." Hazel feared if she asked for anything else, she'd wait forever.

"Great." Belinda hurried off again, and Hazel shifted her gaze to the steaming cup of coffee that she hadn't requested. Good thing she didn't want tea this morning.

She pulled out her phone, figuring she could send a quick email to her mother while she waited for her food, and thereby, kill two proverbial birds with one stone. If she didn't do her weekly check-in, her mother would likely send the witch version of the cavalry after her.

When her orange-flavored French toast and bacon finally arrived, she decided they were worth waiting for.

She'd nearly finished her breakfast when a tall man with olive skin and dark curly hair shot with a few strands of silver approached her table.

"Excuse me?" His cultured, foreign accent was something she hadn't heard since leaving the big city. "Would you mind terribly for some company? There's not so many seats available."

She smiled at his almost-perfect English. "Of course. Please sit down. It seems everyone wants breakfast at Cora's today."

He sat and waved a hand, encompassing the many people in the restaurant. "We're all so happy to be out of confinement and have the sun shining."

"Oh? You were here during the storm?"

His eyes widened. "Yes. Quite a frightful thing with the terrible howling winds and the motel room sounding like it blow."

"It was my first time experiencing it, too. Luckily, my house didn't sustain any damage, just some downed tree limbs, but several in town did."

He nodded to Belinda when she brought coffee and asked if he knew what he wanted. "I'll have what she's having." He pointed at Hazel's plate, and the waitress was off again.

"Excellent choice," she assured him. "Though everything here is very good."

"That has been my experience also." He poured a good amount of sugar into his coffee and caught her raising her brows. "Not like Italian coffee, but this makes it tolerable."

"Of course. No judgment here."

"This wind, it happens every year, yes?" he asked.

"That's what I hear. Supposedly, the persecuted witches who lived here three hundred years ago placed a curse on the town. The storm is a penance they and their offspring will pay forever. According to lore, anyway. Back then, I would guess these kinds of winds and snow would wreak some serious damage. Today, buildings are sturdier."

He blew out a relieved breath. "*Dio e la storia ricorderanno il vostro giudizio.*"

She smiled at the charming man. "I'm sorry. What does that mean?'

"God and history will remember your judgment."

Hazel thought on his words for a moment. "Do you think God will judge those who persecuted the witches or the witches for fighting back?"

He lifted his hand, palm up and shrugged. "I think he takes everything to consideration before he passes judgment. He sees more than we do."

That was certainly true.

She lifted her hand for him to shake. "I'm sorry. I haven't introduced myself. I'm Hazel. I own the teashop down the street."

Instead of shaking her hand, the man turned it and kissed the skin near her knuckles. "Luca Pellegrini."

"Oh," she responded, sounding breathless. She'd never had a man kiss her hand in greeting. "I'm very happy to meet you."

He winked. "This is why Italian men make the best lovers."

She snorted, surprised by his candor and by the fact it didn't come off creepy seeing that he was likely twenty years older than her. "I see."

He shrugged and smiled.

She lifted her gaze as Belinda approached with his food. Beyond her shoulder, Hazel caught sight of Peter waiting by the bar with his hand resting on the butt of his gun. His gaze pierced hers, and her breakfast turned to stone.

How long had he been watching?

She forced a smile and waved.

He turned his back to her, and the bottom fell out of her world. Peter accepted a paper bag from Cora, nodded, and walked from the restaurant without sparing her another glance.

Luca leaned into her point of view. "Is everything okay?"

"Yes, of course." She tried to refocus on her breakfast companion and ignore the sick sensation churning inside her.

She'd done nothing wrong. She hadn't cheated because she and Peter weren't dating. They weren't...anything. She didn't need to apologize or feel bad.

Except traces of his anger and torment still clung to the air.

Luca cut off a chunk of French toast and stuffed it into his mouth. A nod of satisfaction followed. "Excellent," he said a moment later.

She tried to breathe to settle her nerves, but it wasn't working. She might as well accept that she'd be an emotional mess until she made things okay with Peter. Not that she owed him an explanation, just that...

"I'm sorry, Luca. I do need to go. A friend was just in here, and I really need to speak with him. Will you forgive me for deserting you?"

"But, of course. This was not a planned date. There is nothing to forgive."

Hazel stood and was surprised when he did the same. He held out his hand, and she placed hers on his.

"Thank you for the pleasure of your company, bella Hazel." He kissed her hand again and released her. "Perhaps I will see you once more while I am here, and you will bring me back my heart." He placed a hand over his chest in a touching, if dramatic gesture.

She shook her head, but smiled. "Thank you, Signore Pellegrini. If you have a chance, stop by my shop. I would be happy to serve you tea."

He gave her an agreeing nod and smiled.

She turned and walked away. Several people watched her with interest as she left.

By the time she reached the door, she realized she'd done what she always tried to avoid. She'd given enough people in town plenty to gossip about, and now she'd be questioned left and right about the mysterious man as well as about Peter.

CHAPTER NINE

Cool air greeted Hazel as she stepped outside the café, reducing the heat in her cheeks. So much for a celebration morning.

She walked as fast as she could, her feet pounding on the cobblestone sidewalk, straight to the police station. Margaret was off because it was the weekend, and another officer manned the phones. His nice muscles, cropped dark hair and serious countenance reminded her of the enlisted Navy sailors she'd encountered along the coast.

"Is Chief Parrish in?" she asked.

"Yes, ma'am, but he's unavailable." He jerked his head toward Peter's closed door. "Is there something I can help you with?"

Cursed day. She could say it was a personal matter and insist on seeing him, but that would only add fuel to the gossip fires. She shouldn't even care. It wasn't like she and Peter were in a relationship. "Uh, no. Just wanted to see how he liked the latest tea we sent over."

His lips curved, breaking his demeanor into something friendlier. "I like that spiced chai."

She relaxed into a smile. "That's so nice to hear." At least her teashop was running well.

She waved a dismissive hand toward Peter's office. "I'll check in with Chief Parrish another time. Have a lovely day."

"You, too, ma'am."

Angst flared inside her as she headed out of the building and back to the café where she'd left her bike. From there, she pedaled toward home.

With each passing second, her thoughts tortured her more.

She wished she had it in her to walk away, but the thought that she'd hurt his feelings ate at her. He was a good man, and he liked her. She was attracted to him, too. In his mind, there was no reason they couldn't be together.

He didn't deserve to have a crappy day just because she was, and she was left with no way to fix it. Well, she could send a text, but she knew for certain that would do no good. She needed to see him face to face.

Except she couldn't.

She growled in frustration. Instead of taking a right turn toward her house, she went left. Going home would mean hours of replaying the look on Peter's face when he'd spotted her with Luca, which would drive her insane.

Riding would keep her mind occupied and wear her out instead.

As she pedaled, she realized she'd headed directly toward Clarabelle's house and the magical woods. She shouldn't have been surprised. It was Clarabelle's birthday, after all, and maybe this was how she should have spent her day from the start.

She slowed when she reached Hemlock, breathing deeply of the fresh spring air. Birds chirped in the trees, and the sound brought a measure of relief. She cruised across the bridge, casting her gaze toward the sparkling water that flowed beneath. This was such a beautiful area of town. No wonder her ancestors had chosen to live here.

Instead of stopping to hide her bicycle near the bushes alongside the house, she rode all the way to the back where no one on the road could spot her. She dismounted and approached the back door with reverent footsteps.

She expected to catch a glimpse of orange fur creeping up behind her, but Mr. Kitty must have had other more important things to do. Good. She didn't want his energy or anyone else's interfering with her experience today.

The back door was locked the same as the front had been on her first visit.

She closed her eyes and filled her lungs, searching for any sign of a presence. An immediate awareness prodded back.

Hazel smiled and opened her eyes. "Clarabelle?" she whispered though no one was around to hear her. "May I come in? I'd like to wish you happy birthday."

With belief in her heart, she lifted her hand to the doorknob once again. It turned. She pushed on the door, and the hinges responded with a creaky greeting. She kept her heart open as she cautiously stepped inside and closed the door behind her.

Cobwebs cascaded from wooden cupboards to the faded laminate countertops below. Dust motes danced in the sunlight that streamed in from the grimy kitchen window above the sink. A gorgeous, but filthy chandelier hung over an empty space where the table should go. Dusty curtains covered other windows near the table area.

She recognized the place was a disaster, but she couldn't help thinking how beautiful it could be. "You loved this room, didn't you?" she said in a quiet voice.

A rush of warm sensations filled her soul, and she smiled. "I can see why. It's probably hard to see your home in such disrepair, but I promise if I can figure out a way to purchase it without others questioning my heritage, I will. A Hardy belongs in this house."

Prickles erupted along her forearms, giving her a chill. She glanced about the room as though searching for the source of the warning. "Don't worry. I'll be careful."

The cloak of trepidation didn't fade, though.

The first time Hazel had visited Clarabelle's home, a voice had sent her racing off before she'd had time to explore the kitchen.

Now, she had no such worries. She opened a cupboard and inhaled when a black spider rushed into a dark corner, and then promptly closed the door again. She supposed that was to be expected in a house left unattended for so long, but she'd be sure to bring peppermint oil when she returned.

She ventured into the bathroom that had been added on to the back of the house and eyed the clawfoot tub with envy. Obviously, Clarabelle had lived without these improvements, and Hazel wished she could have seen the house as it was when her ancestral grandmother had lived there, happy with her family before disaster struck.

She wandered through the rooms again, catching sight of her footprints on the dusty wooden floors from her previous visit. The warm energy seemed to follow her, and she let it be, enjoying the company. In the room where she'd first discovered Mr. Kitty, she came to an abrupt halt.

No cat prints had disturbed the dust, there or anywhere in the house. A shiver raced over her, leaving her with a tingly feeling. For a moment, she'd wondered if he'd been an apparition or figment of her imagination, but Peter had seen him as well.

She descended the stairs, sat on the bottom step, and opened the secret hiding spot beneath the second stair. Nothing in there but the old wooden box that had housed Clarabelle's book of spells.

"I tried one of your spells that was supposed to make my lashes grow longer. Ended up with purple irises for a couple of days." She snorted at her stupidity and swore Clarabelle enjoyed a laugh at her expense as well.

More? The question echoed in her mind.

"No, I haven't tried more. I'm worried if I use too much magic, someone will discover me."

The air tightened with fear and anger again.

"It's okay." She obviously needed to steer clear of talk about the townsfolk. "I also visited the circle in the grove. It's amazing."

Happiness returned.

"A friend of mine showed it to me. I can't believe such a place exists."

The man.

She froze, a little unnerved that Clarabelle knew about Peter. "Don't worry. He's a good person." Despite his aversion to witches, she believed that to be true.

Yes.

A surprised chuckle escaped her. "Does that mean you approve?"

No answer came, but she had the feeling Clarabelle did. But, would she if she knew his heritage?

"Except I hurt his feelings, and I can't get to him to apologize." She wished he'd show up at the house again or follow her into the grove like he'd done before.

She sighed as the heaviness weighted her heart. "Maybe it's for the best."

Sadness rippled through the air.

"I wish I had a way to learn more about your husband and what happened to him. Where our family went from here."

Book.

"Your book of spells?"

No answer.

Even so, she'd flipped through it enough that she knew it didn't contain a personal history. There must be, or at least had been, another book. Perhaps in the restricted section at the library or hidden somewhere else in the house?

She stood and dusted off the back of her pants. "I wish I could stay here all day, but I should go. That silly orange cat who haunted this place followed me home, and he's likely wondering where I am."

An echo of laughter rang throughout the house. Clarabelle was probably happy to be rid of the pest.

"But I promise to come back often. I like it here. And one day when the time is right, I'll own this house. Until then, keep scaring others away."

The sensation of a caress brushed her cheek, and then the house fell silent and empty once again. Clarabelle had gone. To where, Hazel had no idea, but she was certain the presence had disappeared.

"Happy birthday," she whispered to the silence.

She left the house to find the sun had moved farther across the sky, indicating she'd been inside for quite a while though it hadn't seemed like it. She didn't care. Not many people had the opportunity to communicate with their ancestors, so any time spent with Clarabelle was a blessing.

Back on her bike, Hazel rode the short distance to the bridge, and then abruptly stopped along the side of the road. Sometimes, her ideas were beyond brilliant. She couldn't get to Peter, so she had to make *him come to her.* He wouldn't respond to a simple message, but he would if he thought she needed help.

"Should have thought of this sooner," she muttered as she walked her bike off the edge of the bridge and into the soft dirt at the edge of the pavement. She dropped it there and then half-walked, half-slid down the muddy embankment where she dirtied her hands and wiped them on her knees as though she'd fallen.

She found a perch on a rock and proceeded to do the most embarrassing thing she'd done in her life. Lie for the sake of a man.

CHAPTER TEN

A tirade of dangerous thoughts roared through Peter's mind as he stared blankly at the papers on his desk in front of him. He'd warned the officer on desk duty not to let anyone bother him, and so far, no one had.

That was probably for the best.

He suppressed the urge to roar in anger. He should have stayed at Cora's, should have called out the jerk who dared to put his lips on Hazel. Even if it was only her hand.

Worse, Hazel had smiled. *She'd smiled.* The woman who was so paranoid of being with him, had allowed that guy to kiss her hand. In public.

Peter plowed a hand through his hair, working to regain control of his emotions.

He shouldn't care. Hazel was nothing to him. He wasn't even sure why he'd glanced her way to begin with. He'd managed to avoid a personal relationship with the other women in town. He should have done the same with her.

His cell phone rang, dragging him from his vicious thoughts. He lifted the phone and glanced at the screen. *Hazel.* He spit out a curse and flipped the phone over on his desk.

He couldn't talk to her. Not now.

With each ring, he gritted his teeth and resisted the urge to answer. After a few moments, the incessant ringing stopped.

He exhaled and closed his eyes. Eventually, he'd run into her. By then, he would have had time to close over the wound in his heart. He'd go back to living half alive like he had since he'd laid Sarah in the ground and be just fine. Police work kept him plenty busy.

When the ringing started again, he let go another curse and turned the phone. Her. Again. He ached to throw his phone against the wall and take satisfaction from the sound of it breaking.

Instead, he clenched his fist, scrubbed the side of his forefinger with his thumb, and then growled before he punched the answer symbol on his phone. "What?"

"Peter?"

The sound of her voice tore through the wall he'd begun to erect like a bullet through parchment. "Were you expecting someone else?" He knew it was a crude thing to say, but he couldn't help himself.

"No." Her voice sounded uncertain.

She hesitated for a moment, and his anger started to slip. He couldn't let that happen. "Are you calling to report a crime? If not, I'm busy."

More silence. Then the sound of her releasing a breath. "I need help."

Immediately, his heart jolted into action. "What's wrong? What happened?"

"I did a really stupid thing. I was riding too close to the edge of the road near the bridge on Hemlock. My tire must have caught in the mud. I fell, and I think I reinjured my ankle. I don't know if I can climb back up the incline."

"On my way." Without hesitation, he picked up his keys and strode out the door. "Back soon," he called to the officer, not bothering to wait for a reply.

When he saw her bike tipped at the side of the road, his heart clenched. The thought of her getting seriously hurt or worse was more than he could bear.

He exited his vehicle and hurried toward the embankment. The sight of her sitting on a large rock near the edge of the river brought relief. From what he could see, she hadn't sustained serious damage.

She glanced up with a sheepish smile.

"You okay?" he called and angled his boots sideways as he navigated the slope.

"Just a little banged up and feeling like a fool."

He narrowed his gaze, focusing on the smaller footprints that led toward Hazel. There were slide marks, but whoever had made them hadn't tumbled down the hill like she'd made him believe.

She'd walked.

"Did you fall all the way down?" he asked as he neared the bottom, testing her story.

"Most of the way." She held up muddy palms. "I tried to get back up, but my ankle really hurts."

He was tempted to point out her obvious lie but decided against it. He'd let her talk herself into a corner first and then enjoy the telling.

He reached her and took notice of the smeared handprints on her jeans. "Can you stand?"

"I think so." She got to her feet and then winced.

If nothing else, he could appreciate her acting skills. "Sprained?"

"It feels a lot like last time."

Except last time, she'd been trying to get away from him. "Here. Let me help you." He lifted her right arm and draped it across his shoulder and then wrapped his arm around her waist. Together, they took a step toward the steep embankment.

"It's really pretty here," she said.

He glanced at the arch of the tunnel leading beneath the stone bridge and the clear water running through it. Green buds graced the twigs of trees and bushes all around them. "Sure is."

She gasped as though something had hurt her. "Maybe we should go slower."

They were already moving at a snail's pace. What was her game? Was she trying to delay their movement so she could...what? He doubted she'd apologize. "Let's try this another way."

Before she could question, he bent and placed his free arm beneath her knees, hauling her up against his chest.

"Oh," she said with a breathlessness that satisfied his soul. She could pretend she wasn't attracted to him, but he was as sure of it as the sun coming up in the morning.

"It's okay. I can walk."

"Nope." He tightened his grip on her as he headed for the stones near the edge of the bridge that could be used as stairs. "Best to check out how much damage you've done before you put weight on it."

"But you'll never get up the slope unless you put me down."

The feel of her body against his made it hard to keep his thoughts straight, so he focused on the rush of water passing them. "Trust me. I've got this." He put his foot on the first stone stair and tested his balance before he continued upwards.

"There are steps?"

"Things you learn when you grow up in a town," he offered as an explanation.

At the top, he carried her to the passenger side of the car and helped her inside. He stowed her bike in the back of his car and claimed the driver's seat. His cruiser started with ease.

Neither of them spoke as he drove to her house and parked in front. He exited, helped her from his car, and insisted on carrying her to the front door. He set her down long enough for her to fish the keys from her pocket and open the door.

When he bent to lift her again, she blocked him with both palms facing him. "Thank you so much, but I can make it from here."

He shrugged, pretending she hadn't twisted his insides. "Then I'll get back to work." He left her and strode toward his car. Maybe she really had fallen, and he'd misinterpreted the evidence. Maybe she'd wanted nothing more than a free ride.

"*Wait.*"

That one word was like a hook sinking deep into his gills. He turned to her with a questioning look.

Her expression was alive with uncertainty. "I...Could we talk for a moment? About what happened at the café?"

And there it was. "Doesn't seem like there's much to say."

They stared at each other for several long moments, until the connection between them was almost palpable. "He was no one."

A flash of pain nailed him. "You don't have to explain anything to me."

She stepped toward him, no sign of her earlier limp, stopping when she was only feet from him. "No, I don't, but I'm going to anyway. I went to Cora's alone. You saw how packed the place was. Luca asked if he could sit because there was nowhere else."

She knew his name. "Luca?"

She took his hand, igniting electric sparks between them. "We shared breakfast together. That's it. Yes, we introduced ourselves, so I do know his name. Yes, he was a nice person. But that's it. We sat there fifteen, twenty minutes tops. You can't be mad over that."

She'd shared breakfast...in a public place...with him. "I'm not mad."

"Clearly, you are."

He pulled from her grasp and eyed her. If he didn't spit it out, jealousy would eat him alive. "Okay, fine. Do you want to know why I'm pissed?"

"Yes," she said expectantly.

"Because you'll be seen in public with that guy and not me."

She stared at him for a long, hard moment searching his eyes. "That's different."

He wasn't buying it. "Why?"

"Because he's a stranger. He means nothing to me."

The friction between them shifted, and he could see they both realized what she'd said.

He struggled to keep his emotions from soaring. "I mean something to you?" he asked in a softer tone.

She gave him a small smile and shrugged. "I did let you hold my hand."

He arched an argumentative brow. She wasn't getting off that easy. "You let him kiss yours."

"I didn't let him. He just did. He's Italian."

Peter continued to stare, letting her know he was not pacified by her answer.

"Would you like to kiss my hand, too?" Frustration echoed in her words.

"Maybe." Yes.

"Fine, and then I'm going inside because this has gotten way too ridiculous." She held out her hand.

He wrapped his fingers around hers and stroked her skin with his thumb. So soft.

Slowly, keeping his eyes locked on hers, he brought her hand to his lips. A familiar, delicious sizzle ricocheted through him, and she inhaled a sharp breath.

"It's not enough," he whispered against her skin. Not nearly enough.

She drew her brows together. "What?"

He released her hand and wrapped his arms around her waist, pulling her close. "I said, it's not enough." He caught the flash of understanding in her eyes a second before he lowered his lips to hers.

Sweet mercy.

He kissed her until his lungs threatened to explode. She blinked when he pulled away as though the intensity of their kiss had surprised her, too. He stared at her. His heart thundered. He'd been totally unprepared for how her touch would mess with his head.

Somewhere in there, he found gratification that she hadn't pushed him away or slapped his face.

"I should go," she whispered and stepped back.

"Yes." If she didn't, he couldn't guarantee what would happen next.

She watched him for a long moment, her eyes bright. "Okay." With a deep breath, she turned and strode to her door.

"Take care of that ankle." He sent her a knowing smile.

She glanced at her perfectly fine foot and then met his gaze with a guilty one of her own. She nodded without admitting anything before she disappeared inside.

He swallowed, fighting the urge to follow her, to see her smile, to smell her incredibly soft hair once again. The primal voices inside urged him to claim her, but he fought them. He'd take his time. He sensed they both needed to proceed with caution.

But, whether the woman wanted to admit it or not, this thing between them was far from over.

CHAPTER ELEVEN

The day was bright and sunny, if a little chilly as Hazel pedaled her bike with its basket full of deliveries. She couldn't complain because she was happy to be out in the fresh air, with the nasty storm a week behind them.

She hadn't seen or heard from Peter since the amazing kiss that had upended her world and never should have happened. She'd been unable to sleep soundly ever since, constantly waking from dreams about him.

She'd been eager for her delivery day to arrive so she could return to the Fingleton house, anxious to see if any new leads or information had popped up on the robbery. She'd considered asking Peter but decided against it, so she'd had no news on the burglary coming from that direction.

Sales at her teashop had been bustling with lots of tourists, outsiders driving in to see the damage from the witch-cursed storm. Apparently, that was something that happened every year. Groups of people would argue nature versus the curse, and the talk was enough to leave Hazel's head spinning.

Then there were those who were convinced Ostara was an evil day. She would never understand why people equated a celebration of springtime, rebirth and renewal with something bad. Everyone including the earth appreciated a chance to start anew.

Yes, she knew of devil worshippers who sometimes stole pagan spiritual symbols and mocked them. A few dark witches also remained in existence, but that was no different than the over-the-top, outrageous zealots who came with every religion.

Still, people feared the word, *witch*, especially in Stonebridge.

She passed the library and spotted Timothy Franklin standing in the doorway. Without thinking, she waved. Then she remembered he was one of the haters.

The younger librarian bowed in an old-fashioned manner of greeting, and she smiled, regardless. Although some long-held beliefs were unacceptable, she did appreciate the way the town embraced and preserved historical times.

She believed those touches reminded people to take life slower and remember what was important including family and community. That charm was part of what had convinced her to stay.

A few minutes later, Hazel turned into the Fingleton's driveway and caught sight of Basil as he walked toward the side of the house where she'd seen him the day the pearls had gone missing. This time, though, Sophie was not in sight, and he had his arms laden with bottles of milk.

She pedaled faster and called to him when she neared the house. He turned toward her, a sad frown settling on his otherwise handsome features.

Despite his worn jacket and torn jeans, intelligence sparked in his light blue eyes. After asking around, she'd discovered he'd come from humble beginnings, his grandfather an immigrant from Ireland, but she wouldn't be surprised to see him excel far beyond his family's status.

"Hi there. I'm Hazel Hardy," she said as she rested her bike against the house. "It looks like you and I are doing the same thing." She lifted a tin of tea from her basket as proof.

"Yeah." He started walking along the path that led to the kitchen without giving her his name.

"Do you always take this route? I go to the front door, but maybe Dotty prefers deliveries around back."

"She doesn't want me in her house. She told my father I can still drop off stuff, but I have to leave them by the back door."

"Oh." Dotty's sentence obviously bothered the kid, but she couldn't say she blamed Dotty for feeling insecure. "I'm sure it's just until they catch whoever took the pearls. She's probably letting very few in. Maybe not me, either."

He stopped, and she nearly collided into his back. He turned, and she looked up to meet his gaze. If she were ten years younger, she'd be interested. "No. Even before the necklace went missing, Dotty didn't like me. She doesn't want me around Sophie."

She frowned. Dotty hadn't seemed like the type who'd discriminate against someone less fortunate, though she did remember Dotty saying that she didn't like the way Basil looked at her daughter. But she suspected that had more to do with teenage romance than anything else.

"That seems silly. Aren't you and Sophie friends? Don't you go to school together?"

He nodded and cast his gaze to the ground. "Yes."

Still, her intuition told her there was much more he wasn't saying. "But you like her as more than friends?" she prodded.

He clenched his jaw and then turned a hardened gaze to her. "Friends is all we can ever be."

Her heart wrenched. The poor kid was in love and believed status would keep him and Sophie apart. "I know this town sometimes acts as though we live in a world several hundred years ago, but times have changed. There's nothing to say—"

"I'm sorry, Miss Hardy. I need to go." He turned and strode toward the back of the house, unwilling to listen to her hopeful words.

She sighed as she watched him leave. If he truly loved Sophie, she hoped he wouldn't give up. In a few years, once he graduated high school and experienced the real world, everything could change for him.

She turned and made her way to the front door since Dotty hadn't arranged for her to make her deliveries any other way.

When Dotty answered the door, dark circles and pale skin warned Hazel that she hadn't fared well during the past week. "Hello, Hazel. Please, come in." She stepped back to allow her entrance.

Hazel gave her an understanding, half-hearted smile and entered. "I've been thinking about you every day and hope you're doing okay."

Dotty wrapped the sash on her robe tighter. "I'll admit it's been difficult. I have no idea who I can trust now. My kids are at each other every minute, and I wish I could run away."

Hazel put a commiserating hand on her arm. "I'm so sorry. I wish I could help."

Dotty attempted a smile. "Your tea is the only thing that soothes my soul. I just made a pot of oolong for me, Sophie, and my sister. If you have a minute, why don't you come say hello?"

"Of course." Hazel followed her back to the kitchen and greeted June and Sophie. Out of the bunch of them, June was the only one who seemed unaffected. Dotty was a wreck, and Sophie's red-rimmed and watery eyes proved she was still upset as well.

Hazel took a seat along with Dotty while June fetched another cup.

"I just saw Basil outside," Hazel said and waited for the reaction. "He left your delivery for you by the back door."

Sophie's gaze jumped to the kitchen window, but Hazel was sure the young man would be gone by now.

June snorted in disgust. "I don't know why you allow that thief on your property."

"He's not a thief," Sophie demanded, fresh tears springing to life.

Dotty brushed a strand of unkempt hair away from her face. "We don't know that he's the one who took them. Let's let the police do their job."

"Of course, he is," June argued. "I don't know why the chief insists on looking at anyone else. He's the only one with access to the house who needs the money."

Hazel's assumption of Basil's issues with this family hadn't been far off the mark. "Being poor doesn't automatically make you a thief. Basil seems like a good kid willing to work for money."

"See?" Sophie agreed, flicking her gaze between the two older women.

"Regardless." Dotty eyed her daughter. "You need to stay away from that boy."

"He's not a boy," she defended.

"That, he isn't," June agreed. "Which is another reason why he needs to keep his distance."

Dotty dropped her face into her hand. "I shouldn't have allowed him here in the first place."

Hazel's heart broke for the three women. "How about we let this argument rest for the moment and have some tea? It seems you all could use a break before you break."

"If Sophie's upset, that's her fault," June said. "Her attitude is also making things worse on her mother."

Sophie shot a shocked and hurt look at her aunt. "This isn't my fault. I'm just as worried about that necklace as she is. It's my inheritance after all."

"One that you'd sell in a heartbeat, missy," June countered. "You're acting like you care about the pearls, but you're just mad your mom won't let your boyfriend inside the house."

Sophie's jaw dropped, and she stayed like that for several long seconds. "You, Auntie June, are a horrible person. If anyone stole the pearls, it was you. Everyone knows that you hate my mom because she got them, and you hate me, too, because I'll get them after her, and *you never will.*"

Her words bordered on hysterical by the time she finished.

Sophie stood so fast that her chair fell backward. She rushed from the room sobbing, knocking into Chief Parrish as he attempted to enter the kitchen.

"Whoa," he said, but Sophie didn't slow down or apologize.

CHAPTER TWELVE

Peter turned to the remaining three women, and Hazel's stomach proceeded to tie itself into a perfect Celtic knot. "Sorry for the intrusion. Scott let me in and said I could find you in the kitchen."

"It's fine." Dotty wiped tears from her cheeks. "I'm sorry about Sophie's behavior. She's really upset over this. Please, sit with us and tell me you have some news."

June folded her arms and looked away as though annoyed by the interruption.

Peter took the seat next to Hazel. His leg bumped hers, sending an addictive pulse of energy through her. Even the briefest, innocent touches affected her in a most disturbing way.

"Tea?" Dotty offered.

"Is it Hazel's?" he asked.

Dotty flicked a glance between the two of them and managed a smile. "Of course."

"Then, yeah. That would be great." He waited for Dotty to fill a cup, and then he thanked her with a nod. "Hazel's tea turned me into a tea snob. I never even liked it until recently. Tried a different brand when I was in the city the other day. Awful stuff."

Hazel's cheeks heated. "You're too kind."

"It's true," Dotty agreed.

June released an impatient and very rude sigh. "Do you have news for us or not?"

Chief Parrish turned to her with a shrewd smile on his face. "I'll speak with Dotty in a moment, but first, I have a question for you, June. I overheard the conversation as I walked in, so I'll ask. Where were you the night before and morning when Dotty first noticed her necklace was missing?"

June put a hand to her throat and gasped. "Me? You think I did it?"

He shrugged. "Everyone is a suspect until proven otherwise. Do you have an alibi during that time?"

"You know I live alone," she accused.

"So, you don't then?" he pressed.

June folded her arms again and glared at him. "Fine." She paused for a long moment. "I do have an alibi."

Peter shot her an impatient look, his expression one of a man comfortable commanding attention. "I'm not a mind reader, June."

Hazel sensed the pleasure he took from backing June into a corner, and she couldn't say she blamed him. The woman could be particularly nasty at times and didn't seem to be supportive of her sister or niece.

"Harold Kensington."

Dotty's brows drew together in surprise, and a hint of a smile ticked at the corner of Peter's mouth as though he'd known of her relationship with Harold all along.

"He can verify your whereabouts that morning?"

June's face reddened, and she glared at the chief. "Yes."

"And the night before?"

"Yes." June's answer cut through the tense air.

Peter pulled out the little notepad and pen he carried. He flipped open the pages and held the pen above the paper. "Let me be clear.

Harold Kensington can verify your whereabouts from Tuesday night all the way through the storm until Thursday morning."

Hazel refrained from snickering. She truly appreciated June's business at her teashop, but she couldn't say she minded watching her get a little of what she was so good at giving.

"Yes, Chief Parrish." June no longer contained her anger. "Harold was at my house the entire time. He slept both nights next to me in my bed. Do I need to be clearer?"

Dotty gasped. "*June!*"

Hazel cast her widened eyes downward and tucked in her lips as the urge to chuckle grew stronger. Once again, the not-so-pristine side of Stonebridge reared its head.

Peter finished writing and tucked away his notebook. "Thank you, June. I'll follow up on that. Hazel, I need a word with you before you leave, and then I'd like to speak to Dotty."

Hazel lifted her brows, realizing she was the center of attention. She'd enjoyed watching Peter work, loved the way he came across as a strong and confident officer of the law. But now that his discerning gaze was directed at her, little electric pulses ignited her blood, and she was sure they colored her cheeks.

She scooted back her chair and stood. "Uh, sure. That works for me." As much as she'd love to hear what would transpire between Dotty and her sister, she was done being in the spotlight and weary of hiding her attraction to Peter.

He stood, too. "I'll walk you out."

She didn't complain when he helped her with her coat, figuring it would draw more attention if she did. He walked her to the front porch and closed the door behind him.

Nerves fluttered in her stomach, and she was hesitant to meet his gaze after what had transpired the last time they were alone. But he wouldn't dare kiss her here.

Would he?

She looked up, wondering what he had on his mind. Her breath caught as it always did when she gazed into his mesmerizing green eyes and found attraction burning there. "Is something wrong?"

"I wanted you to know I did a little research on your friend, Luca."

She rolled her eyes. "He's not my friend. He's a person who needed a place to sit, and we shared a meal."

"And he kissed your hand."

She was tempted to tell him he'd kissed it twice but decided the brief satisfaction from stating so wouldn't be worth what might come afterward. "It's customary in his country. He meant nothing by it."

Peter lifted his brows, unconvinced. "I saw the way he looked at you."

Hazel sighed, growing impatient with their conversation. "We've been over this. Was there something you wanted to tell me about him?"

"It appears your friend has a criminal history. Stolen historical artifacts."

Her mouth dropped open. She was certain she looked ridiculous but that was the last thing she'd expected to hear. *"What?"*

"Priceless paintings. But antique pearls that were a gift from King William isn't that far of a reach."

She shook her head, trying to absorb her surprise. "That's crazy."

Peter inhaled and puffed out his chest. "You might want to stay away from him."

The smug look on his face aggravated her. "Did you check up on him because he was with me?"

He didn't appear remorseful for abusing his police power. "I like to know who's in my town. It's part of my job."

"Then you research everyone who doesn't live here? What about the guy who offered to buy Dotty's pearls the day of the storm?"

His look turned incredulous. "What guy?"

"A broker of some sort. I didn't catch his name. I thought Dotty would've told you."

"Well, she didn't, and neither did you."

Her irritation compounded. "Isn't that your job as a detective, to wrangle information like that out of people?"

His gaze narrowed. "Not funny."

She'd pricked his annoyance, but it wasn't enough to satisfy her ire. "How about me? Did you research me when I arrived?"

The change of expressions on his face suggested he'd finally caught on to the fact that he might have overstepped his bounds when it came to her life. "I can't help it if I want to keep you safe from strange men who pass through town."

"And I appreciate that. But, I was in a public place and don't feel like I was in any danger. I have no artifacts for Luca to steal."

He rested a hand on his hip, just above his gun. "No, but checking on him might lead me to the thief. Can't feel sorry about that."

"Hmm..." She nodded. "No, that would be a good thing. But, I'm also not going to feel sorry for enjoying my breakfast that day. Thief or not, I found him charming."

She flashed Peter a brilliant smile and turned, heading toward her bike. "Why don't you check with Dotty or Cora about that stranger?" she called over her shoulder.

And leave me alone, she thought as she walked away.

The man was far too good at what he did, and she hadn't liked that he'd one upped her. Besides Luca *was* charming, and despite what Peter believed, she'd sensed no malice in his spirit.

She blew out a breath of frustration and climbed onto her bike. She needed to stick to tea and leave men out of her life. They complicated everything.

CHAPTER THIRTEEN

Hazel groaned when she spotted trouble peeking in the windows of her shop two days later. An engaging, very handsome Italian man headed toward the door. Luca stepped inside, and his smile blossomed when he caught sight of her.

"Bella Hazel. There you are, my heart."

Even knowing he was a criminal, she couldn't resist his charm. "Hello, Luca. I was wondering if you'd stop in, or if you'd already found what you came to town for and had left."

He placed a hand over his heart as though wounded. "I could not leave without seeing your beautiful face once again. Besides, you said you would serve me tea. I would very much like to taste your tea."

A surprised laugh tumbled from her lips. The man had a way of making everything a romantic gesture. "Then you shall. I have a cozy corner set up over here where customers can try different blends to see what they like."

She eyed him as they walked. "Do you have a particular flavor you enjoy?"

He grinned. "I will enjoy whatever you give me."

She had no doubt he would. If only she could live her life that carefree and happy. "Then I shall choose my Sweet and Spicy tea for you."

A sexy smile turned his lips. "Sweet and Spicy? I like it. Tell me more."

"It's a black tea enhanced with warm notes of cinnamon and sweet bursts of orange. If you were a tea, then I think this is what you would taste like."

He lifted his brows, interested. "Would you like to taste me to find out? A small kiss, perhaps?"

She laughed at his candor and charm, and shook her head. "I only serve tea."

He shook his head in mock disappointment. "That is unfortunate."

Such a charmer. "Have a seat Mr. Pellegrini, and I shall satisfy your taste buds instead. Also, we have cookies from Cora's, if you'd like one."

He sat in the same chair Peter had not that long ago when she'd shared tea with him, and he leaned forward to examine the plate of cookies. He chose her new favorite, the orange-cranberry, and then sat back to relax and watch her prepare his tea.

"This place suits you," he said after a minute.

She brought his teacup to him. "I like to think so."

He gestured with his hand, encompassing the room. "It has a wildness and beauty about it."

"You think I'm wild?"

He caught her with his engaging eyes. "I think there's part of you that's untamed, but you're holding her back instead of allowing her to be free."

She waved away his comment and took a seat across from him, pretending he hadn't hit the mark dead center. "I'm sure we all have a little of that in us."

"Perhaps so." He sniffed the tea and nodded. "Do you have sugar?"

She chuckled. "Try it first. You might find you like the tea as it is."

She'd been tempted to whisper a few words or add a little magical herb to it. Something to ensure he'd love it, or perhaps something to encourage him to tell her if he'd taken the necklace, but her gut told her to keep this relationship pure.

Not to mention, she'd never practiced any truth-telling spells. She'd heard they were unreliable at best.

He hesitated and then sipped. After a moment, he nodded. "It's good, but maybe just a little sugar."

She smiled and threw her hands up in defeat. "Hard to tame a sweet tooth."

After she retrieved the sugar bowl, she was pleased to see that he added only a little and not tons like he had with his coffee. She could be okay with that.

They both sipped tea for a few moments in comfortable silence. Despite what Peter had said, she liked talking to Luca and enjoyed his warm aura. She wasn't attracted to him, as she suspected he wasn't truly to her, either. But she enjoyed his flirting and pleasant nature.

"I have a question for you, Luca."

He lifted his chin, indicating he was open to it.

"You have somewhat of a reputation." She paused, waiting for his reaction. She was surprised when he smiled.

"Are you referring to my prowess as a lover, or my expert skill in acquiring beautiful treasures?"

She couldn't be afraid of this man if she tried. "The latter, actually, though I don't doubt you have many ladies you've left behind with broken hearts."

He sighed. "Alas, it does happen. What is your question, bella?"

She might as well put it right out in the open since he didn't seem to be afraid of honesty. "We had a theft in our quiet little town around the time of the big storm."

He nodded. "The pearls. A gift from King William, dating back to the late sixteen-hundreds."

"Yes," she said, thinking she shouldn't be surprised he knew so much. Maybe Peter was right, and he was the thief. "Did you take them?"

"No." He held up a hand to keep her from interrupting. "Though I am sure they are lovely. However, jewelry does not make my heart beat. I prefer paintings, sixteenth century, mostly, and beautiful women. And although the owner of the pearls is a lovely woman, her jewels do nothing for me."

Hazel choked mid-swallow and then took a sip of tea to clear her throat. "That's very...candid of you."

He shrugged as though she shouldn't have expected otherwise.

"If you didn't take the pearls," she continued. "Then why do you know so much about them?"

"Just because I do not collect that type of history, does not mean I do not appreciate it. The entire history of your town fascinates me, and my nephew has always spoken highly of it, which is why I decided to visit after concluding some business in Boston."

She leaned back in her chair, unsure what to make of the man. She couldn't pick up even the tiniest bit of dishonesty or deception from him. If she had to bet, she'd say he was a man of his word. Which made no sense, except it did in his case. "Your nephew, does he live here?"

"He does. Lachlan Brogan, perhaps you know him?"

"I can't say that I do. His name sounds Scottish." Not at all Italian.

Luca tilted his head and shrugged in a carefree manner. "What can I say? My sister married a Scot. I tried to explain the benefits of choosing an Italian husband, but her heart told her something different."

History showed time and again that love refused to stay within boundaries.

A few moments passed before he spoke again. "Do you believe me?"

She nodded and smiled. "Actually, I do."

"Good." He returned her smile. "It would break my heart if you didn't."

The bell on her front door chimed, and she stood. "If you'll excuse me for a minute, I'll check on my customer."

She turned and saw who was at the door and mentally muttered every bad word she could think of. She strode forward with a smile on her face. "Chief Parrish. Good to see you."

He waited to speak until she'd reached him. "This looks cozy."

"Please don't start again. At breakfast the other day, I told him about my shop and invited him to visit. That's all."

He narrowed his gaze and studied her eyes. She opened her soul to him, hoping he would sense that she told the truth.

He blinked. "Regardless, I'm glad I found him here." He pushed past her and strode toward Luca.

"Peter." She hurried to keep up. "Don't start trouble."

Luca glanced up from his tea as Peter approached. He must have sensed something was amiss because he set his tea aside and stood. "Hello." His greeting was cautious.

"Luca Pellegrini?"

He nodded.

Peter rested his hand on the butt of his gun, and Luca flicked a glance toward the weapon. "I have some questions for you."

Luca's stance remained relaxed. "If it's the same question bella Hazel asked of me, the answer is no. I did not steal the pearls."

Hazel silently asked the Blessed Mother to keep the men's heads cool.

"Why should I believe you?" Peter asked.

Luca kept his gaze focused on Peter, and Hazel sensed his caution and unadulterated awareness. But not guilt. "Because I am innocent. If you have something to prove otherwise, I would very much like to hear it."

Peter held his gaze for a long, uncomfortable moment and then exhaled. "Nothing at the moment."

"Then I'm free to go?" Luca asked.

Peter jerked his head toward the door. "Don't leave town."

Luca nodded in agreement and stepped toward Hazel. "Thank you very much for the lovely tea, my bella." He held her shoulders and leaned in to kiss both cheeks. "I am very jealous of the man," he whispered before he pulled away.

He winked, and she could say nothing as she watched him stroll out the door.

CHAPTER FOURTEEN

Y ou don't have to be so rude to my customers." Hazel avoided Peter's gaze and busied herself cleaning up the cups from her and Luca's tea.

"What did he say to you?" Peter demanded. "What did he whisper in your ear?"

When Hazel had everything loaded onto a tray, she turned and faced him. She'd considered lying but had decided the truth was her best option. "He said he was very jealous of you."

She walked away and headed toward the sink she had in the back room. The sound of Peter's boots indicated he was right behind her.

"Did you tell him about us?" he asked, his tone softer now.

"I told him nothing regarding you." She set down the tray and began to unload it. "Because there's nothing to tell."

Several more moments passed before he sighed. "I don't want to fight, Hazel."

She turned and pinned him with a hard gaze. "Then stop bullying your way into my life and assuming things that aren't true."

"I'm not assuming he's a felon. I'll show you his mugshot if you'd like."

"I believe him when he says he didn't steal the pearls." She waited for the explosion, but it didn't come.

"I wish I could nail him for it, but unfortunately, new evidence has come to light that suggests otherwise."

Her anger faded as curiosity took over. "What did you learn?"

He shook his head, disappointment heavy in his eyes. "Basil skipped town yesterday. Didn't go home after school. His parents have no idea where he went. We found brochures for Canada in his bedroom and put out an alert in case he tries to cross the border."

She put a hand over her heart as sadness welled inside. "No. No, that can't be right. He was a good kid with a good heart."

"He pretty much damned himself by running."

"Stupid kids. Why do they do things like that? I would have bet my life he was innocent."

He met her gaze with an innocent one of his own. "Maybe you're not the best judge of character after all."

The frustrated breath she expelled turned into a growl. "If you're going to insult me, you can leave."

"I'm just saying..."

She looked away from him, letting him know the conversation was over, and pointed toward the way out.

When he tried to engage her again, she shook her head.

He remained for a few more moments, and she wondered if she'd have to ask him to leave again.

"You'll see that I'm right, and that I only want to protect you," he said and then headed out of the backroom. A few seconds later, the bell on the front door rang, telling her he'd left.

Tears of frustration threatened, but she quickly buried them. She couldn't let him get to her like that. Or let her heart betray her when he was around. Logic said he was no good for her. At all.

Her heart needed to listen.

Hazel had managed to collect herself by the time Gretta showed up for the afternoon shift. Instead of staying and crafting tea, Hazel made excuses that she had errands and things around the house she needed to accomplish. Which she did.

But first, she needed ice cream.

CHAPTER FIFTEEN

Hazel sank into the back-corner booth at Cora's Café. She was grateful the place was quiet and would most likely be so until the dinner crowd arrived in a couple of hours.

"Hey, lady." Cora smiled as she approached. "What's up with you this afternoon? You seem a little down."

"I need ice cream."

Cora narrowed her gaze and studied Hazel closer. "That sounds serious."

Hazel blew out a breath. "It is. Chocolate. A big bowl."

"Sounds good. I'm ready to get off my feet. Mind if I join you? Belinda can handle the customers."

Hazel wasn't sure she wanted company, but she didn't have the heart to say no. "Sure."

A few minutes later, Cora returned with two giant bowls of chocolate ice cream. "Too much?" she asked as she set one of them in front of Hazel, the creases in her cheeks deepened by humor.

She shook her head. "I don't think so." And then they both laughed.

They ate several bites in companionable silence before Cora spoke. "I'm going to guess man trouble."

Hazel snorted. "Why do you say that?"

"There's only one thing that will make a girl eat that much ice cream."

Hazel pointed her spoon at Cora's bowl. "You have that much, too."

Cora burrowed her spoon in for another bite. "Cause my love life sucks, too."

She thought back over the past months since she'd moved to town and couldn't recall seeing Cora with a man. "I didn't know you were dating anyone."

"I'm not." She grinned. "That's why it sucks."

She studied Hazel for a moment longer. "But for you, I'm going to say your current mood has something to do with one handsome police chief in town."

Hazel rolled her eyes and shook her head. "Does everyone know?"

"Pretty much. Or at least they're guessing." Cora leaned closer to Hazel and whispered. "I have some special insight, though."

Prickles erupted on Hazel's skin, but she kept her reaction in check. "Insight?" she asked in a lowered voice and then ate another bite.

"Some people can read others better than most, and I can read you."

Hazel swallowed the large lump of ice cream in her mouth, and it struggled to move down her throat. "How so?" she asked when she could.

"Oh, sugar." Cora peeked over the tops of the booths and sank back down. "Did your mama not ever teach you how to conceal better?"

"*Conceal?*" Did Cora mean what she thought she did?

"Wow. Okay." Uncertainty hovered in Cora's wide eyes. She expelled a large breath. "I'm going out on a very dangerous limb here. If I'm wrong, and I'm betting I'm not, I pray you'll keep my secret, but I think I know a kindred spirit when I meet one."

Hazel held her breath, afraid and excited at the same time.

Cora locked eyes with her, and Hazel sensed something prodding her soul.

Her friend leaned forward. "You're a witch like me, aren't you?"

Hazel put her hand to her mouth to keep from gasping. Her heart thundered as every cell in her jumped for joy. "Yes," she whispered and hoped she hadn't just made a deadly mistake.

Cora beamed. "I'm so glad that's finally out in the open."

"How did you know? Because I didn't conceal?" Her thoughts tumbled out in a whispered rush. "I don't know how to do that. We never had to hide in the city. Oh, Blessed Mother, can others tell who are witches? *Could they know?*"

Cora's lips curved into a comforting smile. "You're okay. Don't panic. You obviously haven't used many spells since you've been here. No reason to think anyone else knows."

Hazel shook her head. "I've only created a few potions and one disastrous glamour spell. I've been too scared."

"That's probably a good thing, but don't worry, even I wasn't sure that you were legit until I saw that darned orange cat hanging around your house."

"Mr. Kitty? What does he have to do with anything?"

"That's no regular cat, dear Hazel. If the lore passed down through the years in our families is correct, that cat was Clarabelle Hardy's familiar. Apparently, he's finally decided to take on another witch. No one believed he ever would."

Seriously? Hazel placed her hands together like a steeple and rested her mouth on them. This was all so much to take in. "Clarabelle's familiar? Are you saying he's been here for hundreds of years?"

Cora shrugged. "That's what the legend tells us. You share the same last name. Maybe you're related."

The words admitting that she was indeed Clarabelle's granddaughter faltered on her tongue. It wasn't that she didn't trust Cora, but... "Maybe."

"That would make sense, wouldn't it?"

She thought for a moment and then shook her head, needing to change the subject. "Maybe he's an offspring. I don't think a cat can live that long."

"Who knows? Either way, you're lucky he's chosen you. He'll protect you and help you."

Hazel snorted, remembering him tripping her and causing her to fall on the stairs. "I think he'd rather trip me up than help me."

Cora swirled another bite of melting ice cream. "Maybe you have to win him over first."

She sighed, wishing she had special insight that would give her a clue about the future. "Maybe so."

"Back to the chief."

Hazel groaned halfheartedly. "I don't want to talk about him anymore. The ice cream was just starting to work its magic."

"Okay, okay." Cora laughed. "You just need to be aware that he doesn't play for our team."

"Yeah. I figured as much, which is why I've been trying to keep him at arm's length." She paused. "And failing miserably."

"I have a simple spell that will help hide your magic from him. I'll give it to you before you leave."

Like a neighbor giving her a recipe. "That would be great. Thank you." Having a friend in town had lifted a weight she hadn't realized she was carrying.

"Even so. Be careful. Okay?"

Hazel nodded. She intended to be very careful. "You said *our* team. We have a team? People I know?"

"Probably." She scrunched her features. "You have to understand, though. People aren't very forthright with their secrets. If the wrong person learns their identity, it could cost them their lives."

"But we're all witches."

Cora shook her head, a sad expression on her face. "There are those who might betray us. Always be careful. If the time is right and it's okay with you and some of the others who I trust, I'll let you both know. But I'd need their permission first, too."

"Of course." She hesitated as another thought slithered into her mind. "Do *they* have a team? The other side?"

Her brows shot up. "Oh, yes. Which was why I felt I needed to say something to you."

"Peter?" she asked and held her breath.

"No, I don't think so." Cora's eyes teased her. "Or at least he hasn't shown himself to be. But Timothy Franklin at the library. Mr. Winthrop who died recently. Samuel Canterbury. Those are the ones I'm pretty sure of. There's likely others."

Timothy? That wasn't a huge surprise after listening to his comments. He'd been friendly at the library when she'd asked for books about the historic witches, but she wondered now if he'd been testing her.

One thing was for sure. She wouldn't ask to see the special tomes any time soon or do anything else that might draw attention.

"Good to know. Thank you so much for telling me." She grabbed a strand of hair and dragged it across her lips as she thought. "Aren't you going to ask why I don't just leave town?"

Cora shook her head and shrugged. "Crazy as it sounds, we all have our reasons for staying."

CHAPTER SIXTEEN

By the time Friday morning rolled around, Hazel had firmly decided to cool things between Peter and her. This back and forth attraction and irritation wasn't worth her sanity or her safety as a witch. She wouldn't seek him out, even if it meant she'd be cut off from information on the robbery.

Gretta could take all following deliveries to the police station. If she happened to run into Peter in town, she'd be friendly but avoid all flirtation and leave the scene as soon as possible.

With that settled, she hopped on her bike and headed toward work, grateful that she loved what she did for a living.

Sophie stopped her before she reached her shop and motioned her into an alley between two old brick buildings. Tears stained the girl's cheeks, and her aura held a frantic, worried quality. "Can I talk to you, Hazel?"

She couldn't help but absorb some of the anguish. "How can I help you?"

Sophie blinked, wet eyelashes sticking to each other. "Basil said you were a friend."

"Yes. I'd like to think so. Do you know where he is? I can help."

She shook her head, and her chin quivered. "I don't know. He left and didn't tell me anything. I've been so worried that I can't eat or sleep."

Hazel's heart opened. "You love him." If she hadn't known before, she did now.

Sophie gave several quick nods. "I know he loves me, too. But now he's disappeared."

Hazel took her hand and tried to give some comfort. "Some think he ran off with your mother's pearls."

"No, he wouldn't do that. He's an honest man." She snorted. "Too honest. I think something has happened to him."

Hazel startled. "Why would you think that?"

Her tears started afresh, and she put the back of her hand against her mouth until she could regain a semblance of composure. "I know the police have been looking for him, and I heard they found a body."

Sophie crumpled against Hazel's shoulders and sobs erupted from her. "Worse, I think I'm pregnant."

"Oh, Bless—" She coughed to cover her blunder. "Bless you, honey." She patted Sophie's back and didn't try to stop the flood of emotions.

"What am I going to do?" she wailed.

Hazel pulled a tissue from her purse, lifted Sophie's chin, and handed the tissue to her. "First, you're going to breathe because if you are pregnant, this isn't good for the baby. Second, let's not panic. Until we've received confirmation, let's not freak out and assume the body is Basil's. It could be any number of people."

Sophie released a shuddering breath. "I can't help it."

"I know." She linked her arm through Sophie's. "Come with me to the teashop. I have something that will help calm your nerves." She'd come back for her bike later.

Hazel sent Gretta home for the rest of the day, even though she could tell her assistant was eager to stay and listen. But Sophie deserved the privacy.

When she had her settled and her last customer had left the shop, Hazel claimed a chair next to hers. "Feeling any better?"

Sophie sniffed and nodded. "A little."

Now that Hazel had Cora's concealing spell, she'd been brave enough to add a touch of her special calming potion to the poor girl's tea. "Good to hear."

Hazel relaxed into her chair and sent Sophie a warm smile. She yearned to ask a few questions but didn't want to turn on the waterworks again. "You say you know Basil wouldn't steal. Are you one-hundred percent sure?"

"I'm as positive as I can be. He's not like that. Besides, I asked him to run away with me already. I have plenty in my trust fund to cover us until he can go to school and get a good paying job. That's what he always wanted, you know."

"Why do you think he wouldn't run away with you?"

She wiped tears from beneath her eyes. "I don't know. I wish he would have. He said my family would never accept him, but I told him I didn't care."

Maybe he wasn't ready to be a father. "Did you tell him about the baby?"

"No, I hadn't missed a period then."

"What about your brother?"

A hateful expression contorted her features. "He's the worst out of all of us. If he had taken them, it wouldn't surprise me. Did you know he hasn't been studying while at school? He's failing."

"Really?" Hazel straightened in her chair.

Sophie folded her arms and scowled. "Sounds like a perfect motive to me. He owes money for gambling and drinking. And he would be the type to steal from his own mother."

"I sense a 'but' in there." Which was disappointing.

"He says he's already paid off his debts and has a job lined up for next semester."

Hazel's impression of the kid rose. "That's good then."

"If you believe him. I'm not convinced. If he ended up in jail, I'd never have to see him again. No heartbreak there."

"Do you no longer suspect your aunt?" Since Hazel hadn't been talking much to Peter, she hadn't heard if June's alibi had checked out. "Sounds like she's had her eye on them for a long time."

"Oh, yes." Sophie widened her eyes and nodded. "But that guy did give her an alibi, and now, my mom won't quit talking about how shocked she is that her sister has a lover."

Hazel shrugged. People had a right to be loved and to be happy. "Maybe they were in on it together?" she suggested.

Sophie's expression brightened. "I hadn't thought of that. It would make sense."

Hazel longed to go to Peter and mention the idea to him. "Maybe you should tell the chief. It could be worth examining. Obviously, your aunt's prints would be in the house, but maybe Harold's are there, too."

Sophie bounced on her heels. "You might be right. I'm going to head to the police department right now. Thank you, Hazel."

"Maybe Chief Parrish will have some news on Basil, too."

A look of hope blossomed on her face. "I really hope so."

CHAPTER SEVENTEEN

Hazel took advantage of the warmer Sunday sunshine to take a walk in her favorite woods. Up until now, she hadn't had a chance to visit the spot Peter had shown her because the weather hadn't cooperated, or it had been dark by the time she'd closed her shop.

The carved-out place in the grove that witches had obviously used as a sacred space had now been taken over by teenagers playing with satanic rituals and asking for trouble. She might have to see about cleansing it and warding it with something that would scare the daylights out of the kids so they'd never come back.

Her feet crunched on pinecones as she walked, which released an earthy scent that purified her soul. She ached to go to Peter, to ask what he thought of her and Sophie's idea about June and her man, to reassure him he had nothing to worry about where Luca was concerned, but also to tell him he needed to respect her boundaries.

She sighed and shook her head. This was all too impossible. She was crazy for trying to think of a way to make something work that never could.

Keeping her distance was the smartest choice, if not the easiest.

A spot of orange dashed across the path ahead, surprising her. She narrowed her gaze to see him better. This might be her chance to see if Mr. Kitty was stalking her, or if two similar kitties existed.

She sidled closer to get a better look.

"I see you," she called out in a sing-song tone when she was a hundred feet away. If not for the turquoise collar around his neck, she wouldn't have been sure, but, dang it. That was her cat. "What are you doing here?"

He meowed in response as though she would understand.

She put her hands on her hips. "If you were Clarabelle's cat and have lived for hundreds of years, then you've had plenty of time to learn to speak my language."

Another sassy meow told her exactly what he thought of that.

"Okay. Whatever." She started walking again, trying to ignore him. It wasn't like she could control what he did anyway. Cora's suggestion of trying to win him over seemed ridiculous. She'd given him shelter and food, but he'd never let her close enough for them to get comfortable with each other.

How else could she win him over? She wasn't buying him a mouse, if that's what he wanted.

Mr. Kitty kept his distance but never let her out of his sight. She wondered if that was supposed to comfort her or scare her.

By the time she reached the sacred clearing, the walk had rejuvenated her soul. Unfortunately, the battle between her heart and brain waged on. She sat on the bench where she and Peter had talked before and searched for traces of Peter's essence. He'd said he'd been here many times, so...maybe.

But nothing.

She stood and circled the area, whispering beneath her breath to remove what negativity she could, but erasing all evil would take something stronger. Perhaps a bonfire of white sage to clear it. Although how she'd get away with that, she wasn't certain.

For now, this would help.

"Hazel."

She yipped, covered her mouth, and whirled around like a wounded cougar that had been cornered.

The sight of Peter standing at the edge of the woods, not more than ten feet away, pricked a hole in her defiance and deflated her like a sad, withering balloon. "Peter. You scared me."

His gaze traveled the path she'd just walked. "What are you doing?"

She swallowed and worked to keep her heart rate steady, wondering how long he'd watched her. Wondering why she hadn't sensed him. "Nothing. Just walking."

"In a circle?"

She shrugged and slyly searched for her cat who conveniently seemed to be missing. "The clearing is a circle. Following the edge is easy and lets me think about other things."

He studied her as he strode forward. "I'm glad I found you here."

"Are you following me now, too?" She should have kept her words less antagonistic, but she couldn't help herself.

His smile stole her defenses and warmed her insides. "Yes, I am. I drove past and spotted your bike, and I'm really glad I found you here."

"Why?" She tried to keep some emotional distance but failed. She'd considered parking her bike behind the house again, but hadn't. And this was why. Deep down, she missed him.

"I've been a jerk."

That surprised her. "You have? I mean, yes, you have. You have no right to interfere in my life."

He took her hand. "Sit with me?"

The reconnection with him further soothed her soul. She followed him complacently back to their bench. The smooth wood was cool against her bottom as she sat next to him. No worries, though, because the look in his eyes heated her right up.

"I'm sorry if I get jealous," he said. "You know I like you, and I can't help it."

He held up a hand before she could reply. "But I'll try, okay?"

His eyes mesmerized her, and her anger evaporated like rain on hot pavement. Her heart cheered even as her brain shook its head in disapproval. "Okay." She smiled.

They sat in silence for a moment, but Hazel couldn't stand not knowing. "Anything new in the investigation?"

He chuckled. "I knew you were itching to ask."

She gave his thigh a soft punch. "Then why didn't you tell me?"

His smile widened. "I should have."

"Did Sophie come see you and tell you about our theory?"

"Yeah, but no-go. Harold volunteered to be fingerprinted, and no matches were found at Dotty's house."

She dropped her gaze, focusing on a dried leaf left from the previous autumn. "I hate to think it, but I'm starting to believe it might be Basil. He had access. Motive if you consider poverty a motive."

"We found Basil."

She shifted on the bench to face him better. "You did? Where?"

"Working for a factory outside Boston. We questioned him, but the guy seems clean. I doubt someone who'd just made off with a fortune would be living in the hovel he was. But he has plans for school, and I think he'll be all right."

"If he didn't do it, then why did he leave? He and Sophie were in love. She told me yesterday she thinks she's pregnant."

He rubbed his knuckles across his chin. "If that's the case, that's not good, because he tells a different story. Sophie's in love with him, but he's not so much with her. At first, he was flattered that a pretty, rich girl liked him. He didn't mention that they'd slept together, but he said she'd started talking about marriage and running away within a month of their first kiss. He wasn't ready for anything that serious. Heck, they're both still kids."

Hazel let that information seep into her brain. "I remember coming upon them outside, and him telling her no, too, though I didn't know the context. But she did mention to me that she wanted to run away with him. She said she'd told him that she had enough in her trust fund to support them while he went to school and then found a good job."

He leaned back and furrowed his brows. "Sophie doesn't have a trust fund, Hazel. We investigated the whole family thoroughly, looking for motives, etc."

Hazel blinked. "Then where would she get the...money?" The last word fell quietly from her tongue. "The necklace. She stole her own necklace."

"It wasn't hers, yet," Peter said pointedly. "But let's go with that theory. If she took them, how would she sell them? She doesn't have access to buyers. She's a kid."

She snorted. "Kids can be very resourceful."

She paused as another memory clicked in her brain. "Now that you say that, I remember she was there the day that stranger approached her mother wanting to purchase them for an anonymous client. He left his card. She could have taken it."

Hazel drew a strand of hair across her lips as she tried to recall more details. "Did you ever discover who he was and contact him?"

"Yeah, it didn't pan out. He left town before the storm hit, and he had gas receipts to prove he was back in Boston an hour after he left Stonebridge. We placed him on the bottom of the suspect list."

Hazel lifted her brows in excitement. "But now..."

"Now, we'll be taking a second look to see if that's how Sophie offloaded them." He grinned, and a spark of desire shot through her "Excellent detective work, bella Hazel," he teased, using Luca's pet name for her.

She narrowed her gaze in warning. "Don't be too smug. We haven't broken the case yet."

"Soon." He stood and held out a hand to help her up. "I should probably get right on that tip, Miss Hardy."

"Of course, Chief," she tossed back.

"Can I hold your hand again?" He lifted hopeful brows.

"I'm not sure I've forgiven you, yet." She had, but he could wonder for a while. Still, she didn't pull her hand from his.

He tugged her closer. "Pretty please?"

She groaned as a traitorous smile curved her lips. "Fine. You may."

They strolled back through the bright afternoon sun and discussed the evidence again to make sure everything added up. When they reached the edge of the grove, he released her hand, and she assumed he was trying to honor her request that they not be seen together in public.

His efforts warmed her heart.

She turned to him. "Thanks for a fun afternoon."

He chuckled. "Solving crimes?"

"You know I love it."

"Me, too." He flicked his gaze between her eyes as chemistry sizzled between them.

She should turn and run while she could. But she wasn't that smart, especially not now that she had the concealing spell to help hide her heritage.

Instead, she stood on her tiptoes and pressed her lips to his.

It took him a moment before he wrapped his arms around her, and she liked to think that was because she'd stunned him.

His lips were warm on hers and sent everything inside her tingling in the most wonderful way.

When she pulled away, the bewilderment on his face was priceless. "I thought we were in hiding."

She gave him a casual shrug. "Cora says everyone already knows anyway."

He snorted in disbelief. "Are you kidding me? That's what I've been telling you."

"Well," she said matter-of-factly. "I didn't believe you. Now, I do."

He pulled her in for another kiss that left her breathless. "There. Now everyone really will talk."

She laughed, knowing there was no one around to see except maybe Clarabelle and Mr. Kitty. "Let's not go overboard."

"All right," he said, happiness radiating in his expression. Then he frowned. "Is that your cat?"

Hazel widened her eyes in horror and slowly turned. "Uh...yes, it is. He likes to come to the woods, too." She groaned internally at her lame response.

"You bring him with you?" Incredulity coated his words.

"He likes to ride in my basket." She steadied her gaze on Mr. Kitty and strode forward with purpose. He watched, his green eyes intense, but he didn't move. When she reached him, she bent and wrapped her arms around his soft, furry body and held him close to her heart.

She couldn't believe he didn't fight her or at least hiss considering all their previous interactions. But he held still as though he was as content as could be.

Invisible threads wove between them, surprising her and connecting her to him in a way she hadn't experienced before.

She turned to Peter with a smile, praying Mr. Kitty wouldn't suddenly decide to scratch her eyes out. "See?" She moved to her bike, put him in the basket where he settled, and she climbed on.

"That is one strange cat." He chuckled. "Take care of your crazy feline, and I'll call you later when I know more."

"You'd better. As soon as you find out anything."

With that, she climbed on her bike and started pedaling. She flicked her gaze between her cat and the road. "Thank you for that," she whispered.

He blinked and nodded his head as though he understood every word.

CHAPTER EIGHTEEN

The call from Peter came several hours later, interrupting Hazel's early evening, lazy-day meditation. She grinned and answered the phone. "That was fast."

Peter chuckled. "Surprisingly so, for once."

The happiness in his voice set off her sensors. "Does that mean you have information?"

"Yes, ma'am. I do, but I need your input. Feel like going for a drive?"

She glanced at the clock. The hands were bumping up against seven, but she had nothing else scheduled for the evening. "Sure."

"I'll pick you up in ten."

She laughed at his confidence. "It sounds like you're holding your information for ransom, and the price is a romantic drive."

"Whatever it takes, Miss Hardy."

The sexy way he said her name tempted her heart. "Moonlight and intrigue. How can I refuse?"

Peter arrived two minutes early, but she was ready. He'd said he had important information, and she was dying to know what it was. She opened the door but stepped outside instead of inviting him in.

"Hi." Her voice echoed with breathless excitement, but she couldn't help it.

He was still in uniform, looking as fit and handsome as ever. A sexy smile warmed his features. "Well, hello."

She took his hand and started walking toward his police cruiser. "Tell me what you learned."

He tugged her to a stop and twisted her until she was in his arms. "Anxious, are you?" A teasing smile played on his lips.

She squeezed his arm. "I wouldn't be if you'd just tell me."

He watched her with a narrowed gaze, but she sensed his teasing manner. "I'm starting to wonder if you like me only as an informant."

She snorted. "Of course not. I only like you because you carry a big gun."

His eyes grew wide, and he laughed. "You know what that sounds like, right?"

She turned a sassy smile on him. "Nope. No idea."

"We'll talk on the way." He opened the passenger door for her, but she stalled.

"Give me a hint first."

He lifted his brows in victory. "We located the broker and received confirmation of what we expected. Now, get in."

Her pulse spiked with excitement. "Really?" She wasted no time climbing onto the passenger seat.

Peter entered on his side, started the car, and put it in drive. He glanced over at her as he drove. "I shouldn't act so happy about this, but I'm relieved to have proof."

Fresh air blew in from the open windows and caressed her skin, igniting her senses. "It is Sophie, right?"

The mood in the car dropped, then, and he sighed. "Yeah, it's her. She contacted the broker just as he was leaving Stonebridge before the big storm. I'm guessing you were right thinking she'd snatched it."

That made sense. "Then the pearls had actually been missing for a couple of days before Dotty noticed."

He tipped his head in agreement.

Hazel's disappointment in the girl spread like tea overflowing a mug. "What a shame. Poor Dotty. She's such a nice lady and deserves better treatment from her daughter."

"Yeah." Peter drove on back streets as the sun faded in the sky. He turned onto a side street that curved deeper into the trees, leaving the sights and sounds of the town behind. With the sunlight blocked, dark shadows surrounded them, giving the illusion of a secluded sanctuary.

Not too far in, he pulled to the side of the road and killed the engine. "Care to get some fresh air? I've been cooped up in an office far too much lately and need to stretch my legs. There's a decent walking trail here."

A stroll in the fresh evening air? Like she'd ever say no to that. "I'd love to." Connecting with the elements grounded her like nothing else.

Hazel smiled when he took her hand and they set off. "Did you know walking is good for thinking? It helps access both sides of the brain, letting you process things better."

He squeezed her hand. "Is that right?"

"Yep." She accidentally kicked a small rock and sent it skittering ahead on the trail. Wandering off into thick trees, like they were, at the edge of dusk might not be the best idea, but she had her protector with her and that made all the difference.

He slowed their pace when they reached a spot where the banks of the nearby stream bumped close to the trail. Water trickled and sang with the creatures of the evening, lulling her into a relaxed state. Scents of wild honeysuckle drifted through the air, igniting her senses to a higher vibration.

Nights like this pulsated with pure magic and set her soul dancing.

He tugged her toward an old log near the bank, and they sat. "Next step is to focus on getting her necklace back." Weariness echoed in his voice, making her yearn to help him.

"It sounds like Sophie still has the money because she was planning on using it to run away with Basil. I don't think she realizes when he left, he was running from her."

Peter twined his fingers with hers and traced the underside of her forearm with his free hand. "I would agree with that."

Delightful shivers raced over her skin, and she fought to concentrate on the case. "So, if you can recover the money from Sophie, you can give it back to whoever bought the jewels—"

"June."

"You're kidding?" She shifted until she faced him directly. "June is the mysterious buyer?"

"Yep, and the second she learned she'd purchased stolen property and said nothing, she became an accessory."

Hazel's shoulders sank and she blew out a defeated breath. "Oh, wow. This will kill Dotty."

"It's going to be tough on her, which leads me to my next conundrum. The broker is currently out of the country, and while he did give us the information we wanted over the phone, he was clear he'd be reluctant to testify at trial. I threatened to subpoena him, but he said he'd be a hostile witness, and that was if we could find him to deliver the subpoena." He snorted. "Apparently, revealing discreet details about his clients would kill his business."

Hazel placed her hand over his to still his movements and give her a chance to think. "He's lucky he's not going to jail, too."

Peter continued to trace small circles with his thumb. "Exactly. For Dotty's sake, I'd like to keep this quiet."

"Then, it sounds like the best possible outcome would be to have them both confess."

"That's what I was thinking, too. Any ideas on how to achieve that, Sherlock?"

She squeezed his forearm in protest to his teasing. Though really, she thought she'd make a fine detective if she ever decided to switch professions. "You want me to figure out all the hard parts, huh?"

He shrugged nonchalantly, but she sensed the teasing inside him. "Why do you think I let you hang around me?"

She gasped and gave him a token elbow in the ribs.

He grunted though she knew she hadn't tagged him that hard. "Really, though. What do you think? Any ideas?"

She turned toward the stream so she didn't have his handsome face distracting her and tried to focus. "Hmm…. What about a cozy family meeting with all the players there? Give them a couple of details and let them squirm before you sock it to them."

"Sock it to them?" He chuckled. "You're starting to sound like a true Stonebridge citizen."

His comment made her smile. "Whatever."

"Yeah, whatever," he teased. "I like the idea, though. I'll call Dotty and set it up."

She ached to watch the whole thing go down. "Can I come, too?"

"You'd be so disappointed if I said no, wouldn't you?"

She did her best impression of sad puppy dog eyes and made him laugh. "You know I would."

"Fine. On one condition."

Her excitement spiked. "What?"

He drew his thumb down her cheek, generating myriad shivers. "You'll let me steal another kiss."

"Isn't extortion illegal?" she teased.

He shrugged, his gaze laser focused on her eyes. "I don't care."

Instead of answering, she placed her palm on his cheek and stretched until her lips kissed his. He might have thought she was sacrificing for what she wanted, but she didn't see how she could lose in this situation.

Hot guy. Sweet kiss. And all the intrigue.

CHAPTER NINETEEN

Late the next evening, Hazel knocked on Dotty's door, her nerves a tangle of anticipation and excitement. When Dotty answered though, her eagerness dropped to apprehension. "Hi, Chief Parrish told you I was coming, too, right?"

"He did." Dotty stepped back to welcome her in. "He said he has news for us."

Hazel was happy to see that Dotty had dressed and done her hair that day, and that she seemed in a much better place than the last time Hazel had visited. She worried that Dotty's next rebound would take much longer after the reveal that night.

She followed Dotty into the sitting room where she found Sophie, Scott and June already seated on the couch and flanking chairs.

Sophie's gaze connected to hers, and she drew her brows together in question. Hazel offered a kind smile in return. Poor girl, even though she was guilty. She'd thought Basil loved her, and she'd likely gone so far as to commit a crime to ensure she'd have a future with him.

Love was nothing to trifle with. It could lead a person down a dangerous road just as easily as it could make her happier than she'd ever believed possible. That was always the risk where love was concerned.

"Why are you here?" Scott asked. The deep frown on his face proved the emotions she'd previously picked up were correct. He was in a dark mood, and though he might be innocent of theft, he had other sins to atone for.

Hazel shrugged. "Chief asked me to come."

The doorbell halted any further questioning. Dotty left the room. When she returned, Chief Parrish followed her. He looked so handsome in his uniform, sure and confident. She should add sexy. So sexy.

The familiar pang of longing rolled through her when her and Peter's gazes briefly connected. He didn't smile like he usually did but acknowledged the rest of the people in the room instead. "Good. Everyone is here."

Dotty perched on the edge of the couch, expectation vibrating from her. "You said you have news on the robbery. That you believe you've found the thief."

Peter nodded. "Yes, I believe so."

Hazel slid her gaze to Sophie who watched Peter without flinching. Her gaze was steady enough that Hazel began to second-guess their conclusions. She could detect no guilt, or really, any emotion.

She flicked a worried gaze toward Peter, but he was focused on Dotty.

He claimed a chair across from Hazel and pulled out his notebook. "Let's start with Basil."

June snorted in disgust. "I knew it."

Peter lifted his gaze. "Knew what, June?"

"That he's guilty," she spat. "Worthless, no good—"

"Stop!" Sophie cried. "It wasn't him."

Peter nodded. "Sophie is correct. It wasn't Basil. It also wasn't the infamous Luca Pellegrini, known thief and all around bad guy." He slid his gaze toward Hazel.

She gave him a smug smile that he ignored.

"In fact," Peter continued. "The thief actually sits among us."

His declaration sent emotions in the room skyrocketing.

Fear.

Anger.

Disbelief.

Sophie pointed at her brother. "You did it."

Scott's dark mood deepened. "Did not, loser. Everyone knows it has to be you."

Sophie gasped. "Why would I steal it? It's going to be mine someday anyway."

June sank deeper into the pillows on the couch while Dotty's face blanched. "Someone in my family stole it?" she asked Peter with emotion coloring her voice.

"I'm afraid so."

Dotty looked at each of them, anguish hovering in her eyes. "Who?"

None volunteered his or her guilt.

She looked back to Peter. "Tell me," she demanded. "Who in my family? Who of these people that I love and trust would hurt me this way?"

Scott stood. "I want to know, too. Which one of you guys could do that to mom?"

Peter shifted his gaze to Sophie who grew wide-eyed and fearful. "Not me," she exclaimed.

He glanced at his notebook as though checking information, but Hazel knew it was for effect only. "Were you in a relationship with Basil?"

She glanced between her mother and aunt. Her fear grew strong enough to overshadow the other emotions in the room. "Yes," she whispered.

Peter nodded.

"I knew it," June said again. "He was good for nothing. Did he make you take your mother's pearls?"

Everyone in the room turned to Sophie.

She remained silent and still for several long moments. "Yes," she finally said. "He forced me to."

Peter snorted and slowly shook his head. "That's not really true, is it Sophie? I know it's hard to own what you've done, but it's better to do it now than later in a court of law."

She held her stoic gaze for another few moments and then crumbled. Her eyes flooded with tears. "You don't understand. I had to. It was the only way to be with Basil. No one here would accept him, so we needed to run away. Except he got scared after the pearls went missing."

Sophie inhaled a deep breath and expelled it. "They were going to be mine anyway, so what difference does it make?"

"Sophie." The pain on her mother's face tore at Hazel. "You did this to me?"

Sophie wrapped her arms around her midsection. "I'm sorry, Mom. I had to. I think I'm pregnant."

Resounding gasps echoed through the room. "Pregnant?" Dotty whispered.

Scott's chuckle ran the border between gleeful and disgusted. "I knew it."

Hazel ignored him. "Except didn't you take the pearls before you knew that, Sophie?"

Peter kept his focus on Sophie. "Would you like to tell the whole truth now?"

A sob escaped her as she jerked her gaze to each of her family members as though they'd cornered her and anyone of them could attack at any moment.

"Fine," she said with a shaky breath. "I did it so he'd love me. At least I thought he would. He didn't want to be serious. He said he had nothing to offer someone like me, so I wanted to prove he didn't need to."

Peter nodded. "The pearls were the trust fund you mentioned to Hazel."

Sophie slid a hard look toward Hazel as though she'd betrayed her. Her silent accusation hurt until Hazel realized it wasn't hers to own. Sophie had brought this on herself.

The girl turned to her mother. "I'm sorry. I was so stupid. I thought I could make him love me, but he doesn't." More tears erupted. "He never will."

Scott snorted. "What a bunch of bull. I hope none of you are going to fall for it."

"Sophie," June admonished. "How could you do this to your poor mother?"

Hazel widened her eyes in disbelief. The woman would soon find out she wasn't getting off easy, either.

Sophie buried her face in her hands and sobbed in earnest.

Peter focused a hardened gaze on June, and Hazel inhaled in anticipation. "The second question would then be, June, how could you do this to your sister?"

June's expression exploded in shock, and she lifted her hand to her throat. "What do you mean? I didn't help Sophie steal them."

Peter gave a nod of agreement. "No, but you hired the man she eventually sold them to, didn't you? A broker named Arnie James?"

Dotty swiveled a pained, wide-eyed gaze toward June.

June was up and off the couch faster than Hazel thought possible. None of them had time to react to her response before she was out of the room. The front door slammed, sending the sound vibrating through the house.

"Are you just going to let her go?" Scott cried, pointing a finger toward the empty doorway.

Peter didn't seem concerned in the least. "She won't get far. I have an officer positioned outside."

"Oh, good Lord." Dotty shook her head, and her breaths grew labored. "Betrayed by both of them. I can't... I can't..."

She crossed her hands over her chest, alarming Hazel.

She jumped to her feet and rushed to Dotty's side. "Are you okay?"

Dotty struggled to fill her lungs. "I can't breathe."

Hazel jerked her gaze to Peter for help, but he'd already clasped the radio on his shoulder.

"This is Chief Parrish. Send an ambulance to the Fingleton residence. We have a woman with chest pains."

"If she dies, I'll kill you both," Scott said to his sister.

By the time the ambulance arrived, June and Sophie were in hysterical tears. Both sat on the front porch in handcuffs.

Peter did his best to hold the scene. Hazel held Dotty's hand until the medics helped her onto a gurney, and then she and Peter walked with her to the ambulance.

"I'm so sorry," Hazel said as they prepared to load her inside. "Hang in there. I promise this will be okay."

"Will you come with me?" Dotty croaked. "I have no one else I can trust."

Hazel glanced to Peter. "You don't need my permission. Go with her. I'll take care of everything here."

"Okay." Hazel nodded. Dotty needed her, and she couldn't refuse. She climbed inside and sat next to the female medic.

The woman cleaned Dotty's skin with an alcohol wipe. "We're going to start an I.V.," she said to Dotty in a calm voice.

Dotty looked to Hazel, and she gave her a kind smile. "Just relax. Everything is going to be okay."

Hazel turned to look at Peter, but the other medic closed the doors between them. She wanted to reconnect with him before they departed, wanted to ask when she'd see him again, but there was no time for that now.

Her head knew that she'd see him soon, but her heart ached to know for sure. For now, though, she'd have to focus on Dotty and let the future bring what it would.

EPILOGUE

Hazel lifted a hand-painted ceramic mug from the open box she had on the counter in the backroom of the teashop. She widened her eyes in delight. Delicate pansies circled the middle of the cup in shades of blue and purple with bright yellow centers. Lacy blue detailing along with green swirls edged the top and bottom.

Several customers had requested mugs in which to make a larger serving of tea, and of course, she wouldn't refuse them. Most of what she'd placed on this order were feminine like this one because the largest portion of her customers were female, but she'd also purchased several manly mugs with various shades of blue, green or brown that had a rougher finish.

"Hey."

Peter's greeting startled her, and she almost fumbled the mug. She flicked an annoyed sideways glance at him. "Do you always have to sneak up on me?"

"How else am I going to discover what you do when I'm not around? You had a pretty big smile on your face when you pulled that out of the box."

She shook her head in warning. "You're lucky I didn't accidently hurl the mug at you in self-defense. That would have served you right, and then you'd have to explain to the guys at the station how a woman attacked you with a coffee mug."

She played off his suggestion that he watched her well, but inside, she made a mental note always to stay aware of her surroundings. Although, it seemed unfair that she couldn't let her guard down in her own backroom.

He moved farther into the room. Each step he took toward her increased her pulse in a delicious way, and he stopped near her elbow. "What else ya got in there?"

"Nothing you'd be interested in unless you like daisies and tulips on your cups."

He shrugged. "I might. Not for me, but for Margaret on administrative assistant's day or her birthday."

"Or just bribery to keep her around and put up with you," she teased.

He grinned. "That, too."

She finally gave him her full attention. "What's up?"

"Nothing. I just wanted to see you."

Her heart danced. "You just wanted to see me?"

"And...see if you were in the mood for afternoon ice cream." His hopeful look tugged at her heart. She sensed his attraction, but also that he'd wrangled it under control somewhat.

She hesitated as she stared into his beautiful eyes. If she said yes, their dating would become official. Gretta in the outer room would be the first to know, and she'd never let Hazel live it down.

Her brain continued to list all the reasons saying no would be a good idea, but...

"Okay."

Happiness erupted on his face. "Really?"

"Sure," she said and shrugged as though it was no big deal. "Why not?"

"Why not indeed." His grin was contagious.

She quickly washed the packaging dust from her hands and then turned to him. "Ready."

He took her hand and led her from the backroom. Gretta glanced up as they emerged, her gaze quickly dropping to their clasped hands.

She met Hazel's gaze and widened her eyes.

Hazel buried her smile. "We're going for ice cream. Can you man the shop for a bit?"

A knowing grin spread across her lips. "Sure thing, boss."

She and Peter rounded the counter and headed for the front door. Before he opened it, he looked back at Gretta. "She finally said yes," he said in a loud whisper.

Hazel shook her head at them both, and she was sure she heard a giggle as they stepped out into the beautiful spring day.

They held hands the entire way to Cora's, and Hazel was sure everyone who passed gawked at them, but she didn't pull away. They received similar looks from Cora, and Hazel tried not to let her anxious feelings get the best of her.

"Booth or table?" Peter asked.

A table would leave them more exposed. "Booth."

Thankfully, Peter guided her to a booth near the back, and she slid in.

Without warning, he sat next to her, his thigh brushing hers, sending all kinds of intense energy racing through her. She'd expected him to sit opposite her, but she should have known better.

He reached across her for a menu, and she caught a whiff of his cologne. The man was irresistible. When he opened the menu before them, she glanced down to hide her smile.

"What are you going to have?" he asked.

The nerves in her tummy had twisted into a crazy bunch, and she wasn't sure she could eat anything. "Maybe a root beer float."

"That sounds good."

Hazel sensed someone approaching, and she glanced up. Dotty stood before them with a huge grin on her face. "Look at you two.

I'd wondered if there was something between you. Every time I saw you together, I thought something seemed different about you both."

Hazel worked to think of a good reply.

"Good to see you looking happy, Dotty," Peter answered instead, saving her from Dotty's awkward comment.

"I'm better than happy. I'm great." She looked like she'd recently had her hair done, and the soft lavender blouse and black slacks she wore flattered her figure. She glanced toward the door and her smile grew bigger. "Apparently, cupid's been hanging out around town," she whispered.

Hazel and Peter both cranked their heads around to see who Dotty referred to.

Luca Pellegrini approached them, looking as dashing as ever. "Bella Hazel," Luca said with a lovely Italian flourish.

Her heart warmed with affection. "Luca, good to see you."

Luca gave Peter a courteous, if stiff, nod and turned his gaze to Dotty. "Shall I acquire us a table?"

"Yes, please." Her expression glowed with happiness. "I'll be right there."

"What's this?" Hazel grinned expectantly at Dotty, and she blushed.

"A new chapter in my life. I'm done worrying about and taking care of everyone else who doesn't do the same for me."

Peter nodded. "Sounds like a good plan. I understand you're not pressing charges against your daughter."

Dotty flicked her fingers as though shooing away a fly. "She would deserve it, but I couldn't hurt her that way. She is, however, finishing high school at a religious boarding school and then off to college. It will be a terribly long time, if ever, before I can forgive her. Scott has already gone back to school and won't be home for the summer, either. Selfish brats. Let them learn to survive on their own."

"What about Sophie's baby?" Hazel asked.

"There is no baby. She might have thought she was pregnant, but it was more likely another of her lies." Dotty placed a sassy hand on her hip. "That girl needs to grow up before she even thinks about having a child."

Hazel and Peter both agreed with nods.

"Don't forget to keep that safe locked," Peter said. "And be careful with that one." He nodded toward Luca.

"I already know his history, so don't worry about me. Luca agrees this is all for fun. Don't worry about the pearls anymore, either. I sold them." She laughed.

"Seriously?" Hazel asked, surprised.

"That broker was right. Why should I continue to hold on to them, hiding them where no one will see? Sophie doesn't deserve to inherit them, and I don't want Scott to get them, either. I decided to share them with the world. Now, my bank account is fatter, and I'm going to enjoy the proceeds myself. If my kids inherit a dime when I pass, they'll be lucky."

"That's certainly understandable," Peter said.

"And you know what?" Dotty said with a smile. "It feels wonderful. Now, if you'll excuse me, I have a hot date. My sister's not the only one who can have a man on the side."

Hazel laughed. "You picked a good one."

Peter sent her a disagreeing look but said nothing.

After Dotty walked away, Hazel nudged Peter with her knee. "I think they're cute together."

He snorted. "I think *we're* cute together," he said instead of arguing.

She let that sit in her thoughts for a few moments. "Maybe so."

"You know we are." He lifted the menu and studied it.

She cast a sideways glance at him. She didn't know how cute she was, but he was, by far, the most handsome man she'd met. Not that she'd tell him.

Dangerous, too, she reminded herself. But now she knew how to be careful.

Maybe she'd follow in Dotty's footsteps and keep things fun but casual. It seemed like a win-win, and she couldn't see any other resolution.

Belinda approached and frowned at seeing them together. Hazel smiled bigger.

The woman seemed to think she should have all the male attention in town. This time, she was wrong, and Hazel enjoyed her dissatisfaction more than she should have.

"Are you having a root beer float, too, Peter?" Hazel asked sweetly.

He met her gaze and smiled. "Yes, I think I will."

He turned to Belinda. "Root beer floats for me and this lovely lady."

Belinda smirked and walked away.

Hazel grinned at Peter.

Yes, this dating thing might be fun after all.

* * *

Read on for an excerpt from Book Three in the Teas and Temptations Cozy Mystery Series

* * *

If you enjoyed reading this book, the greatest gift you can give me is to tell a friend and leave a review at Amazon or Goodreads. It helps others find stories they might love and helps me to continue pursuing this crazy writing career.

Thank you and happy reading,
Cindy

Excerpt from THREE TIMES CHARMED

Teas and Temptations Cozy Mystery Series
Book Three

Hazel Hardy entered her living room after a long day at work, teacup in hand, and found a fat orange tabby crouched on her reading chair, watching her with that sassy expression he always used.

The cat, with his odd, mysterious ways, had lived with her long enough to know that after work and dinner, she'd head for her favorite spot to read and relax. He'd proven to her time and again that he had an intelligence beyond most felines, and for that very reason she knew he lounged in her space on purpose.

She strode forward with a stern expression, hoping to intimidate him. She was the boss in this house, and he needed to learn that. "Get out of my chair."

He yawned and regarded her with a bored expression.

She set her cup on the table next to the chair and reached out with both hands, prepared to pick him up and physically remove him from her spot. The moment her fingers were an inch away from his soft fur, he sprang up and ran for the cover of the couch.

She narrowed her gaze. "One of these days you're going to give me a heart attack, and then there will be no one to take care of you." Though, from the looks of him, he'd managed to eat well before he'd begun to stalk her.

Hazel turned to claim her spot, but her ancestral grandmother's ancient book of spells now sat where the cat had been. That little stinker. He'd seemingly managed to open her underwear drawer, dig beneath all her panties and bras, and pull out her grandmother's tome.

Apparently thinking that drawer might be the safest place in the house to hide one of her darkest secrets had been a mistake on her part. She could question how he'd managed such a feat, but that went along with wondering how he'd escaped her house when all the windows and doors had been closed and locked.

Where Mr. Kitty was concerned she'd learned not to question anything.

That didn't mean she would take his sass without giving some back.

She lifted the book and then shot the cat, *her cat,* she supposed, a narrow-eyed glare. "Why is this here?"

The orange tabby stared at her as though he regarded an imbecile.

His attitude did nothing to ingratiate him to her. "Don't you know it's not polite for a man to rifle through a lady's lingerie drawer?"

If she didn't know better, she'd swear he lifted a sardonic brow.

She kept her gaze on him as she moved the spell book to the table next to her chair. She sat and picked up the thriller she'd been reading, instead.

She showed him the cover and smirked. "I don't know why you think you get to tell me what to do in my own house. You're the guest here. I'm the one who goes to work to make the money that buys your food so you can stay fat and sassy."

He let out a long caterwaul followed by several short bursts of meowing that sounded an awful lot like he was telling her off. When he was finished, he shifted a suggestive gaze to the spell book on the table.

She flicked a glance at it and then looked back to him. "No."

Yes. You must.

Of course, he'd pull the creepy mind communication when he didn't get his way. She had so many reasons to boot his orange butt out the door, but this was why she kept him. He knew things she didn't. Things she feared she'd need to know if she intended to stay in the town that had stolen her heart.

Must? Why must she read it? She'd certainly been curious enough when she'd first found it, but the darker than dark spells at the back of the book had left her...uncomfortable.

Her mother had pounded the message to stay away from black magic into her brain so often during her childhood that she'd become annoyed. *We are not the type of witches who tap into that power. To do so is to invite things into your life that you don't want.*

Like she would ever consider messing with danger. She'd lived her whole life using her magic to help and heal people. It wasn't in her to do otherwise.

But she'd also never had it thrust right into her face like this, either. And the whole "must" thing stirred the worry inside her. Stonebridge might look quaint on the outside, but she'd discovered it also had a shadow side, which left her anxious.

She looked back to Mr. Kitty who still watched her with a serious yet annoyed expression. "I've already looked at this. I've learned everything I need to know."

Look again. You need to learn.

"There's nothing in there that will help me with my life. I know all about brews and potions, and I use those in my teas to make people less stressed, fall in love, and feel better. My life is happy the way it is. I don't need to learn anything else."

You need to protect yourself.

His understated warning sent chills skittering across her skin, but she still couldn't honor his request. "No, I don't. I know the rules and the cautions of living in Stonebridge. Cora gave me a concealing spell if I ever need to use magic. Which I don't intend to do."

She wanted Mr. Kitty to help guide her, but not when it came to dark magic.

She pointedly opened to where she had left off reading the thriller, and did her best to ignore the intense energy that blasted from Mr. Kitty's direction. She wouldn't be controlled by a cat. A crazy one at that.

She was in charge of her destiny. "Maybe someday I will want to go back through it, but not now. Today, I want peace and to lose myself in a world of murder and mystery. So, bug off."

If you don't learn, you'll have no peace. Dead or alive, you will find no peace.

Again, his ominous warning stirred the anxiety inside her until it boiled. She growled her frustration at him.

Mr. Kitty crawled from beneath the couch, not threatened at all by her outburst, and jumped onto the coffee table in front of Hazel where he proceeded to look her directly in the eye. *Don't make me tell your grandmother.*

Son of a crunchy biscuit. The last time she was at Clarabelle's house, she'd had something of a conversation with her ancient grandmother's ghost. Hazel had innocently managed to trigger unfounded fears for her grandmother. The last thing she wanted to do was upset her further.

If she didn't appear to try to learn, Mr. Kitty would make sure she couldn't visit her grandmother again without repercussions. Not only that, Hazel intended to purchase Clarabelle's house, and she'd hoped to make a good life there. For that, she needed a happy grandma ghost.

Hazel sighed and shot a disgusted look at her cat. "Fine," she said in a snarky voice. "I will read it tonight, but tomorrow, we're back to the thriller. Understand?"

Her cat watched her until she picked up the book of spells and opened it. Then he jumped off the table, crawled back under the couch, and curled himself into a ball where he would likely fall asleep.

She opened the cover to the front page and caught sight of Clarabelle's quote again. *Better to follow your heart, or you're already dead.*

Had her grandmother meant that in reference to life in general, to a man, or to following the prompting of her heart where spells were concerned? She wished she knew that and so much more.

Except not about her dark spells.

Hazel hesitated, wondering if Mr. Kitty would hear her switch the books again and then decided he'd know if she did. Instead, she flipped to the page she'd marked with a kiddie bookmark she'd obtained from the library.

The Wrath of the Damned.

****

The title of the spell gave Hazel shivers. "The Wrath of the Damned," she whispered. Sounded horribly ominous to her. She supposed that was the point.

This would be the spell that her grandmother had used to create what the residents called the infamous Witches' Wrath. The noreaster storm Clarabelle and her cohorts had created ravaged Stonebridge every year around Ostara as punishment for the town who'd persecuted the them for their beliefs.

On the next page, she found instructions for evaporating water.

A hair from each of the witches.

Blessed water from Redemption Pond. The place where the pious townsfolk had laden Clarabelle's pockets with stones before they'd ruthlessly pushed her and her friends overboard and left them to drown. Her grandmother must have known what was in store and had given survival her best shot.

She wondered if they had tried the spell out in advance, or if the moment they'd sunk to the bottom, they'd had no idea whether their attempt would work.

And worse, what it must have been like to realize they'd failed. The thought left her sad.

Blood of the accuser.

Three simple ingredients. Still, she couldn't help but wonder how they'd thought they could manage to collect blood from their accusers.

She wished there was an easier way to learn more about her ancestor's history. Maybe Hazel needed to reconsider fully reading the book. Maybe then, she'd find clues as to what had happened during those last few days before Stonebridge's citizens had tried and convicted her.

During Hazel's first attempt to read the entire book, she'd smiled at the childlike scrawling that detailed how to find edible mushrooms or how to calm a cow before milking. Those spells included who'd taught them and, frequently, the name was Mama.

As she'd turned the pages, the writing had grown smoother with a distinctive flair that Hazel supposed had been common during that time. Those spells had come from many different sources besides Clarabelle's mother.

Eventually, Clarabelle had become the creator of spells, including the darkest ones that appeared last in the book. If Hazel understood Mr. Kitty correctly, she was expected to learn everything inside, even if she knew she'd never use it.

Not knowing where to start reading this time, she closed her eyes and ran a finger over the edge of the pages waiting for a spark of knowing from the universe. When it came, she slid her fingernail into the space and opened to that page. As she read the words, she drew her brows into a curious and uncertain frown.

From what she could tell, this was a spell for money.

Huh? That didn't seem horribly awful. Like could this make her rich?

The idea appealed to her. If she had to learn something new, this didn't seem so bad. And money, if used correctly, could provide lots of positive outcomes.

A coin as an offering.

Blood from the seeker.

She blocked out her mother's words that warned of anything requiring blood. Blood spells were dark spells regardless of how innocent they might seem.

Then again, her mother had no idea what it was like to be caught between two worlds like she was. Her mom *had* told her to be careful and protect herself. Practicing this spell would likely fall under that category since she knew Mr. Kitty would make her life miserable if she didn't do something.

Burn over the flame of desire until the two become one.

That's it? She could place a drop of her blood on a penny and heat it with fire, and then the universe would grant her more money?

She shut the book with a snap. Mr. Kitty startled and sent her a nasty glare.

Holy harpies. She was so doing that right now. She could be rich by tomorrow. Then she could buy Clarabelle's house and anything else she wanted. How cool would that be?

Just because her mother had only taught her passive spells didn't make all the others wrong. Hazel had a heritage of rich blood in her veins, and it would be a shame not to explore it a little.

She assembled the ingredients in her kitchen. A penny. A pin to prick her finger. A lighter and a pair of pliers to hold the penny while she burned it. This was much simpler than the spell she'd tried in an attempt to grow her lashes longer. There was no way she could get this one wrong.

Before she began the spell, she whispered the words Cora had taught her so that she could conceal any trace of her magic from the world.

"Close their eyes. Cover their ears. Let me practice with no fears. When in this space, no one shall see...the magic that I bring to be. I deem this true, so mote it be."

Then came time for the pin prick. She wasn't one who could easily inflict pain on herself, but one small bit of discomfort would be worth the outcome, right? Even if this spell was blood magic, she wasn't cursing anyone or asking for unearthly power.

Which is what Clarabelle must have done to drain the lake. The thought bewildered her.

Enough procrastination. She placed the pin over her finger and inhaled. With a quick stab, the tip pierced her skin, and she grimaced from the prick of pain. She dropped the pin and squeezed the tip of her finger until the blood welled into a red bud.

Her heart thumped loudly as she turned her finger downward and continued squeezing until a drop fell onto the penny. She carefully secured the penny between the tips of the pliers and then flicked on the lighter. It took a few moments for the penny to heat, but when it did, blood bubbled on the surface.

She cast a quick glance at the tome and carefully repeated the words scrawled on the page.

"A sacrifice is made as my thanks to thee. A willing gift of blood in exchange for money. This wish will be granted, so mote it be."

When the blood became dried rust on the penny, she released the lighter and dropped it on the kitchen counter. The hot penny glowed with energy as she set it on a ceramic plate, and then she paused to study her work.

She didn't feel different, didn't feel richer, and she wondered how long it would take before her spell went into effect. It wasn't as if her phone was ringing with someone on the other end giving her the news that she had inherited a million dollars from a long-lost aunt.

Maybe it was one of those spells that took time. That was fine with her. She had all the time in the world.

Or maybe she'd done it wrong. Or maybe her innocent heart wouldn't allow her to illicit such magic. Either way, she could say she'd tried to learn.

She turned and startled. Kitty was perched on the table, watching with approval in his eyes.

"Why do you have to do that? Can't you be a normal kitty who doesn't maim and scare the daylights out of his owner?"

He chuffed, jumped to the floor, and strode away with his tail high in the air as if to say no one owned him.

She shook her head in annoyance.

By the time she put away her tools, the penny had cooled. She gently picked it up and carried it upstairs with her into her bedroom where she placed it under her pillow. This way, it would be out of sight.

Not that anyone would be in her house to find it. But she'd messed with magic, something she'd promised her mother she wouldn't do once she was in Stonebridge. After what had happened to poor Clarabelle, she wasn't taking any chances.

You can find THREE TIMES CHARMED, Teas and Temptations Cozy Mystery Series, Book Three, on Amazon.com.

Book List

TEAS & TEMPTATIONS COZY MYSTERIES (PG–Rated Fun):
Once Wicked
Twice Hexed
Three Times Charmed
Four Warned
The Fifth Curse
It's All Sixes
Spellbound Seven
Elemental Eight
Nefarious Nine

BLACKWATER CANYON RANCH (Western Sexy Romance):
Caleb
Oliver
Justin
Piper
Jesse

ASPEN SERIES (Small Town Sexy Romance):
Wounded (Prequel)
Relentless
Lawless
Cowboys and Angels
Come Back to Me
Surrender
Reckless
Tempted
Crazy One More Time

I'm With You
Breathless

PINECONE VALLEY (Small Town Sexy Romance):
Love Me Again
Love Me Always

RETRIBUTION NOVELS (Sexy Romantic Suspense):
Branded
Hunted
Banished
Hijacked
Betrayed

ARGENT SPRINGS (Small Town Sexy Romance):
Whispers
Secrets

OTHER TITLES:
Moonlight and Margaritas (Sexy Contemporary Romance)
Sweet Vengeance (Sexy Romantic Suspense)

About the Author

Award-winning author Cindy Stark lives with her family and a sweet Border Collie in a small town shadowed by the Rocky Mountains. She writes fun, witch cozy mysteries, emotional romantic suspense, and sexy contemporary romance. She loves to hear from readers!

Connect with her online at:
http://www.CindyStark.com
http://facebook.com/CindyStark19
https://www.goodreads.com/author/show/5895446.Cindy_Stark
https://www.amazon.com/Cindy-Stark/e/B008FT394W

Made in United States
North Haven, CT
27 June 2024

54155584R00081